SEAN DORMAN, as a boy of
Irish public school, was awarde
and the English master regularl'
Form. He became editor of the
winner of an essay competitior

Great Britain and Ireland. After graduating at Oxford, he worked
as a freelance journalist in London, having articles published in
some twenty British and Irish periodicals. He also ghosted half
a dozen non-fiction books for a publisher. He had a burlesque
of Chekhov staged by the Dublin Gate Theatre, a radio play
broadcast by Radio Eireann, and he published a few short stories,
one being broadcast by the BBC. For five and a half years
in Dublin he published a literary, theatre and art magazine,
Commentary. In England, from 1957 until a few years ago, he
ran the Sean Dorman Manuscript Society for mutual criticism, a
Society still run by others under the same name and listed in *The
Writers' and Artists' Year Book*. His magazine *Writing*, also
listed during its career in 'The Year Book', was founded in 1959,
and sold after twenty-six years. While his family was growing
up, he had to seek a more regular income, and taught secondary
school French and junior German for some twenty-five years. To
make up for lost time, between 1983 and 1993 he wrote and
published, under the imprint of his Raffeen Press, eleven books.
They embraced novels, autobiography, essays, a three-act play,
theatre criticism, short-stories and a solitary poem. Many of the
books were re-writes or extensions, now allowed to go out of
print, so the present tally is six. Five of these have been included
in his three-volume hardback, *The Selected Works of Sean
Dorman*, now gradually finding its way into national and
university libraries throughout the world.

COVER GIRL
For my beautiful Irish compatriot,
FIONA.

Also by Sean Dorman

BRIGID AND THE MOUNTAIN
a novel

PORTRAIT OF MY YOUTH
an autobiography

THE MADONNA
a novel

THE STRONG MAN
a play

PHYSICIANS, PRIESTS & PHYSICISTS
essays

and published by The Raffeen Press

Further copies of
RED ROSES FOR JENNY
may be obtained through
WH Smith, Waterstones and other good bookshops.
Also from The Raffeen Press
Union Place, Fowey, Cornwall PL23 1BY.

RED ROSES FOR JENNY

Sean Dorman

THE RAFFEEN PRESS

Cover montage: JOHN ALLMARK
Photograph: Jim Matthews
Seascape and graphics: John Allmark

BRIGID AND THE MOUNTAIN
A RAFFEEN PRESS BOOK 0 9518119 7 5

PRINTING HISTORY
In paperback 1988
Reissued in three-volume hardback
The Selected Works of Sean Dorman 1993
Raffeen Press reissued in paperback 1995

Printed and bound in Great Britain by Short Run Press Ltd, Exeter.

RED ROSES FOR JENNY

Chapter One

Henry Hampton bustled into the drawing-room to find his wife and son seated one on each side of the large fireplace with its broad wrought-iron grate, and long brass poker and tongs propped up on a pair of brass rests in the fender. The fire, in a bad mood because of damp wood, boiled sulkily, pushing out ill-tempered little wet flames.

His son Jim had been lounging with his long fingers buried for warmth in the fur of the cat on his lap — that fateful cat which was to initiate such dreadful decisions in his father's head. She had been receiving the attentions of a lover. Henry had caught a glimpse of this gentleman in a glossy black morning coat, with white markings on his four paws that suggested spats and kid gloves. He had the air of having just changed into his most dandified gear to go sparking.

Jim had been watching his mother. Her hands were clasped about the warmth of the cosied half-empty coffee-pot. He found himself thinking: she meets the passing years so easily! No over making-up to give an unintended raddled appearance, like some of the others.

Vera Hampton became aware of his blue eyes on her. She looked back at him with eyes of equal blue. With her finger tips she prodded into place a stray lock of her thick brown hair, beginning to grey a little. 'Come on, swap! My turn for the cat.'

They exchanged those two hand-warmers, cat and coffee-pot, glad to be playing again the game that they had played on many a chilly evening.

When Henry had briskly brought in his large frame, the cat had studied him with alert gold-flecked eyes. He stared back at her. She jumped down. While lifting her gently out of the room (cats were

7

for catching mice and not for petting), he noted a small thinning spot on her forehead. He had some ointment; he'd try that.

Jim Hampton stubbed out his cheroot. 'Must be off. Got to put canvases on stretchers. As I said to Rembrandt — or was it Titian? — it's very hard to paint on a limp canvas.'

Vera laughed. 'Go on with you!'

Henry saw the pride in her blue eyes (a wonderful blue, he always thought) as she watched their tall son's lithe step leaving the room. She recalled again that day of his birth in 1911, just three years before the war. Her golden pregnancy . . . The sluggish animality, her husband's ever-present concern . . . The first kicks of the baby in her womb had filled her with wonder at the arrival of a new somebody. The feeling of emptiness at his birth, of the loss of her treasure and of animal intimacy, had been quickly removed when he was on her breast like a big bee. But it was the beginning of his going away from her, for then had come weaning — and he had been going away from her ever since. She picked up her book with a sigh. 'The bird is leaving the nest.'

'I don't catch your meaning,' said Henry (who had caught it very well). He pronounced the word 'catch' as 'ketch', a stray infection, acquired from the surrounding speech of the County Cork, not proper to be found in the mouth of an Anglo-Irish gentleman. Otherwise in the main his accent was impeccably English. His father had, of course, sent him to an English public school, and he in his turn had sent Jim.

He crossed the drawing-room. The chandelier shook icicle-light over the powerful dome of his balding head. He pulled aside a tall curtain and watched Jim cycling down the drive. A sea mist was stealing into the town. The evening sunlight came muted through it. To the west, golden trees banked in the sky. A saffron darkness was beginning to cap the hills. 'Why ken't the boy work at home, instead of wasting money on this so-called studio. I mean to say, there are plenty of rooms here. Now when *I* was a boy . . .'

Vera, to soothe him, changed course. 'Perhaps the process is beginning to reverse itself. Perhaps the bird is beginning to return a little towards the nest.'

'How d'you mean?'

'He's come back from Paris and London. He's gone into the family printing business. He's . . .' There was her son's new attitude of chivalry towards her. 'I wonder if Jenny ever thinks of marrying Jim.'

'Marrying! The girl's only eighteen.' These match-making women! His hand dived into the pocket of his jacket, there arose the rustling of paper, and he popped into his mouth one of those boiled sweets that were the source of his slight fleshiness.

Vera regarded the tremor in his burly form with surprise. 'Jenny reminded me she'd be twenty next year.' Nineteen thirty- five . . . How the years tumbled by! 'You know that very well, old boy.' The 'old boy' was a remonstration.

He rolled the boiled sweet into his bearded cheek. 'Ah, for goodness sake, woman . . .'

'Well, Henry, it would help to keep him nearer home. Someone we knew, at that.'

'The boy must get himself settled in first.' He spoke in the hectoring tone he used to employ to his Indian assistants in the engine-room when they were bungling something. Before inheriting the printing business on the death of his father, he had been a marine engineer out East and so escaped the Kaiser's war in Europe. He had joined a local defence force.

Vera, generally the peace-maker, this time was not to be deterred. 'Jenny has always been crazy about babies.' The young girl seemed to have adopted her as her second mother. Perhaps she sought from her the more personal affection that she lacked at home. Oh, Mildred Byrne cared immensely for her daughter, but . . . Perhaps it was a case of a little bit too much ambition for her daughter; using her as the instrument for the realisation of her mother's schemes.

'There's plenty of time for that.'

'Not for Jenny. Some girls mature young. She would have liked to marry and have children even at seventeen.'

His moustache twitched. 'Jenny has no thought of Jim. Rather, I would say . . . I'm going to bed.'

'Me too. All that gardening has made me weary.'

Upstairs, he stood looking out. The brown scent of fallen leaves idled in through the window. He knotted meticulously the cord of his pyjama trousers. His moustache had ceased to work. You didn't ketch Jenny showing any interest in young men. Perhaps they frightened her. Children, indeed! What nonsense Vera could talk at times! The few street lights along the quay far below were switched on. In the thickening mist, they were burning cores surrounded by haloes.

He turned round to see that Vera, propped up in one of the twin beds, was reading her bible. What a handsome woman she was, her thick brown hair framing her smooth brow! He crossed the room and kissed her. Her lips were soft as ever. In her returned pressure, had there been a touch of warmth over and above her usual fondness? Perhaps this time . . . He kissed her again, cautiously releasing some of the pent-up ardour. There was the same old stiffening of her body and expression of withdrawal.

He sighed and returned to the window. He thought of the comfortable old double four-poster bed, inherited from his parents. In the discomforts of the final stages of her pregnancy, it had been removed to the loft in favour of the two modern single beds. After the birth of Jim, he had chilled at her repeated postponements of its return. He had resolutely refused to sell it. Perhaps Jim would have a use for it . . . Mind you, he had every sympathy for Vera. She was a fine woman, a *fine* woman. He had a deep understanding of her religious and social attitudes, for were they not his own also? But it had been a trial attempting to marry the vigorous sexuality of a robust body to the severe demands of a puritanical upbringing. Small wonder if the coach, drawn by so disparate a pair of horses, had sometimes lurched.

A charming young face with deep violet eyes, set in an aura of light gold hair, floated into his thoughts. Jenny Byrne seemed firmly to have adopted him as her father. Yes, and more, as a — companion. The poor child had suffered in quick succession the loss of her father, and then that of the companionship of Jim when he had gone away. Not that the boy had shown a great deal of interest in her. Couldn't blame him. There were five years between them, and that was a lot at that age. Jenny had been only a schoolgirl. Shy, particularly of men, she clung to her small Anglo-Irish circle. Henry remained as the closest substitute, both as father and friend.

Vera, who had taken up her bible again, was regarding over its top the silhouette of her husband's broad shoulders. Her rejection of him weighed heavily. The spark that made intercourse possible to her, the hope of a second child, had become extinguished with the extinction of that hope. Not even her intense fondness for Henry could replace it. Take herself to task as she might, by stages it had degenerated into a distasteful duty, and then into an impossibility. If he found solace elsewhere, she couldn't really blame him. Not that his religion would allow him to . . .

The moan of the siren buoy Masterman came faintly from beyond the harbour mouth to Henry's ears. He was seeing Jenny Byrne when she was a little child skipping at his side on one of their summer evening walks, her hand holding two of his fingers, her pony-tail flopping up and down on her neck. They had stood aside as the farm dog pushed furious cows, accompanied by a placid curly-coated bull, ahead of him down the lane. Bees drifted through the diamond dust.

'Come to bed, old fellow. You'll catch your death of cold.'

Henry scraped with his thumbnail at the putty. 'Cracking badly. Must get it redone,' he said to the window pane.

He was now seeing Jenny as the young lady of seventeen. It was another summer evening, and this time they had strolled arm in arm, and this time it was through his own garden that the golden bees had blown, colliding with the white martial trumpets of convolvulus on the march. Filtering through leaves, the sun threw leopard skins on the lawn.

He deposited his fourteen stone upon a mattress that received it with metallic protests. He was seeing Jenny Byrne as nineteen (for, in his calmer mood, he admitted to her true age), as his secretary, his right hand in the office. It took him a long time to get to sleep. He dreamt that he was young again. He lay on his back at the edge of a field, in his nostrils the scent of new-cut barley drying in the sun, in his eyes the tree-tops soaring into the blue sky and filled with the voices and wings of birds. A puff of white air, composed of thistledown and grass-seed, ballooned by. Rank heat oozed up from butterfly-rich nettles.

When daylight dawned, it was to a morning of green and grey velvet. The long black fishing-boats slept on the surface of Glenmorris harbour, a surface on which the light from the mist-filled sky, and the long reflections from the surrounding hills, winked alternately grey and green. The images of the hills, and of the white cottages with their dark slate roofs, came to Henry, standing with tall straight back and wide shoulders at his bedroom window, softened through the mist.

He motored slowly through the vapours. It was one of his mornings for arriving late at the office, and Jenny had walked down before him. He was caught up in diaphanous memories that coiled and eddied about his brain, like the grey draperies that withdrew before his progress and closed in after him again.

His eye was arrested by roses — red roses — in a window. On an impulse, he braked to a stop.

'I'll have two bunches.' He flashed his genial smile at the fifteen year old daughter of the house.

She hastened round the counter to supply her eminent customer from the window. He saw that she was wearing a pair of her mother's cast-off high-heeled shoes. Her thin tanned legs were very white just round the ankles, where she usually wore socks.

He remembered that he had on a savings campaign. Many years before he had bought an annuity for Vera. If he died and anything happened to the business, he wasn't going to have her, without a servant, trying to run the huge house and garden on her own. Vera would do anything for the family and close friends, and some of them would perhaps exploit her hospitality. 'No, better just let me have one bunch.' Pennies saved, quickly turned into pounds.

'Only the one! You wouldn't get no better.'

Henry nodded, but his jaw set. 'Just the one.' The annuity had lost value, and he meant to make a further purchase to restore it to its old level.

The girl slowly wrapped a piece of newspaper round their stalks. She sucked at a finger where a thorn had pricked it. According to her mother, Mr Hampton wasn't a man who had to count the coppers.

As the car ran along the quay, two men in blue sweaters and canvas trousers, examining nets on a slipway, touched the peaks of their caps. White boats, their bottoms painted with black varnish, lay upside-down along the seaward side of the rutted roadway. A lone schooner, in the thirties all that was now left of a one-time fleet, lounged against the quay wall, the falling tide having left her insufficient water in the undredged harbour. When he was a boy,

12

the port would have been bustling with coastwise trading schooners and, once a year, the Manx fishing fleet. Grey weather-slated Glenmorris rose up the hillside behind a line of black warehouses of wood and corrugated iron.

He stopped at the end of the quay on the pier. Overhead ran frenzied gulls screaming for fish scraps from men cleaning herring. Their cries, desolate as a stormy sea, answered one another in a wild antiphony. He strode towards the large red- brick building with a board across its face reading: The Glenmorris Printing Company.

As he entered, Mrs O'Donovan, scrubbing the lobby floor with water and Jeyes Fluid, reared up to her gaunt six feet, her tight little grey curls springing about like steel coils. 'Good morning, sir.' She simpered at him down her pink nose. She scrutinised the roses. As he mounted the staircase two steps at a time with long legs that refused to accept age, her eyes were still on the flowers. They nodded their big red heads at her energetically under the compulsion of Henry's movements. She nodded back at them thoughtfully. Well now! 'Twasn't often that one saw roses as fine as them.

He reached a long room with a roof constructed of cobwebs and dirty panes of glass. In the yellow-grey light, he frowned at a young compositor eyeing the blooms. He didn't pay him for idling. The compositor hastily resumed picking letters of type with a pair of tweezers out of pigeon-holes and assembling them into advertisements, captions and titles. An older man, his nostrils flaring, presided like a demon over a hissing monotype machine tapping out columns of hot lead. The floor in the centre of the room yawned in a great well. Leaning on the protective railing which surrounded the well, Henry inspected the Hades below with an engineer's eye and ear. Imps in white overalls hovered about machines, turned by belts clacking over pullies, that spewed out sreams of printed matter.

Through the panes that formed the top half of the partitions of his office, he was able to look into his son's. Had the boy overslept in that attic studio of his? But, in the office beyond, Jenny's shoulder-length hair, whose brightness so contrasted with the deep violet of her eyes, fell over her cheeks as she typed. Charming! Just to look at her made him feel young again, and happy.

He crossed the empty intervening office. 'Good morning, Jenny.' He attempted a tone of as much playfulness as a racing pulse would allow. Must have come up the stairs too quickly. He brooded on that air of hers that so intrigued him, alternating between a spirited independence and an intense concern for people.

'Are those for the office?' Dodo had never brought in flowers before.

His genial smile failed a little. 'For you.' He watched her young face struggle between incredulity and delight. He thrust out the flowers to the full length of his tweedy arm. 'Here, ketch hold of them. Mind the thorns.'

She leaned back languidly a moment, watching his eyes on her breasts. The discovery that her body was a weapon had made it harder to resist the charms of passivity. But of course in *his* case there was no question of that. Of course not. It was just that she liked to bask in his admiration. She rose. If it was pleasant to have a god standing before her in homage, it wasn't pleasant to insult his superiority by keeping him so. She felt enveloped in his rough tweedy power, in the authority of the grey hairs streaking his dark beard. She put out her hand for the flowers.

Her dimpled knuckles and tapered fingers enfolded the protecting piece of newspaper. Her full first finger made him think of a penis. He wished that her warm palm was holding, not the stems of flowers, but . . . He roused himself with a start. His voice became severely practical. 'Jenny, would you just ring the Customs in Cork. Find out if that art paper has been landed yet.'

At the cold douche, she too seemed to start out of a dream. 'Yes.' She moved towards the door. As she passed him on the way to the telephone in his office, she buried her face in the blooms. Then she put her hand on his shoulder and kissed him lightly on the cheek.

At the window, Henry stared at the long grey ramparts of King William Fort crouching at the far side of the harbour, and at the grove that stood nearby. His square fingers stroked his beard. The sun, in a fit of aggressiveness, burst through the mist and started drinking it up.

'Dad, I shan't be asking you to drive me up to dinner tonight. Mum knows. Jenny's taking my place. I have to finish the last of the pictures I'm exhibiting in Cork.'

'Exhibiting!' Henry stood at his own office window. Long tongues of shadow were beginning to invade the October sunshine. A *little* drawing, in so far as it helped the boy's design work in the printing office, yes. But what was the good of all this arty-crafty stuff? His expression relaxed. He would be driving up Jenny alone! Well, it was only understandable that the boy should want to complete his work. After all, easel pictures *were* sold, often for very good prices. There was that Rembrandt . . . 'All right, Jim, if you insist,' he said in a tone of good-humoured resignation.

Jenny's violet eyes were observing the two men. Her fingers fiddled with the vase of roses on her desk, their big red faces brightening the drab office. Standing there so tall and waistcoated, so blue-eyed and cherooted, so intelligent and lithe, Jim had something of the authority of Dodo himself. And always there hovered at the back of her mind the 'necessity', as her mother constantly assured her, for marriage and children. The reflection was killed by a stab of hostility. Jim had been indifferent to her in the past. Well, she would be indifferent to him too.

Not that Mummy had any need to preach! Jenny had dreamed of marriage and motherhood almost since her first doll. Well, motherhood anyway. During one of her rebellious moods, she had questioned the necessity for a husband. Mummy of course had been horrified. Jenny had not persisted. She herself was deeply involved in Glenmorris and its people, or at least in that little Protestant Anglo-Irish colony, in the midst of the Catholic majority, that constituted her people. She could never wish to offend them just for the sake of giving offence. In fact, that was something actively to be avoided unless overriding principles were at stake.

Though, half an hour later, Henry's eyes were set on the narrow winding streets through which he was driving (how one wished to reconstruct several of them, getting rid of quite unnecessary kinks; he must bring the matter up at the next meeting of the Urban District Council), he was vividly aware of the tender rounded shape and delicate skin of a neck warmed by the October evening. As he left the shops and houses of Lower Glenmorris behind and began to zigzag up the hill, he felt it safe to detach one hand from the wheel. He drew her against him. An emerald field stretched away into a powder-blue distance, with a few trees standing upon it in the gloaming, feathery statues.

Vera, her graceful neck clustered with Indian beads, waited on the doorstep. 'Hello, you two!'

She watched them advance, Henry looking handsome in his dark blue seafaring cap set at a jaunty angle. A sudden warm little wind lifted and fell. The dry leaves rattled down from a tree. There came sailing on the breeze a great host of thistledown, feathery balloons, each balloon its charge a single seed. Some of the down caught for an instant in Henry's beard, or lodged upon his broad shoulders. His arm was about Jenny. As she pressed her shoulder lightly against his chest, she seemed slight against his tweed- jacketted immensity.

Vera assumed surprise; it was her way of administering a reproof. 'Have you only just arrived? Dinner's been ready a quarter of an hour.'

Jenny's feet, shod in high-heeled shoes old but becoming, stepped out languidly in the deep gravel. How nice it was to have a second mother in Vera! Not that there was anything wrong with Mummy. Mummy was certainly devoted to her good, and very ambitious for her. But . . . If only she'd sometimes kiss her or put her arm round her. 'I *do* like your new dress.'

Vera laughed and started down the stone steps towards them. Her heel caught. She fell her full length on to the gravel.

Henry was beside her in a stride. 'Are you all right, darling?'

Jenny put her hand to her mouth. She hastened after him.

'It's nothing. I didn't really hurt myself a bit.' As she herself always worried about her family, she assumed that they would worry over her. And indeed Henry always did. Suspicious of enjoyment, he certainly didn't suspect suffering. The sick were the especial children of God. 'It's just' — she drew in her breath — 'my ankle.'

'Why ken't you be like Jenny,' he grumbled gently, 'and manage high heels better? Here, ketch hold of me.'

By the time that Jenny reached them, Henry had already raised Vera as though she were no more than a feather. Jenny made to support her on one side, but found herself excluded by Henry's arm. His brown eyes, turned solicitously upon his wife, seemed to have forgotten everything else. As husband and wife made their way towards the door, Jenny stood alone on the gravel staring after them.

Coming out from dinner, prepared and served by Bridie, the

cook-general, Vera said, 'Henry, take Jenny into the drawing-room. I don't like leaving the coffee to the tender mercies of Bridie.'

He nodded genially. 'Come along, Jenny.'

She regarded his big fingers about her wrist. 'Oh Vera, do show me how you make your coffee. It's always so much nicer than anyone else's.'

With a deft movement she had withdrawn her arm. She slipped to Vera's side. The memory of that surprising emotion on the gravel disturbed her. Was it — jealousy? Rubbish! Absolute rubbish!

'I *am* very particular about coffee.' Vera's voice had a modest inflexion. The world of men was stimulating, but it was a harsh world. It was nice to have, in the softer cosier world of women, a sympathetic and intelligent companion, even one so much younger, with whom to discuss recipes and by whom to have one's dress admired. Henry often admired her hair when she had a new style, but he wasn't good on dresses.

She began to limp her way towards the kitchen. Instantly Henry's moustache changed from the twitch of being ruffled to the twitch of concern. 'Now look, Vera, you go and sit down. Bridie can get the coffee.'

She laughed fondly. 'My ankle hardly hurts at all. Jenny'll give me a hand.'

'You'll go knocking yourself up,' he grumbled. 'I know you.'

In the drawing-room, he switched on the chandelier. He went the round of the four tall windows, drawing the long ruby curtains. Far down below, the harbour stretched away in a vapour of stars. He lifted a folding table over to the fire and fixed up the flaps. He put out two packs of playing-cards and a scoring pad. His gold fob watch, also inherited from his father, was produced and put to his ear. No sound of footsteps from the kitchen. There was an empty interval of time, of life, which must be filled with activity. Plants in the greenhouse required watering. He could just squeeze it in.

When he re-entered the great front hall, filled with such necessary objects as spears, elephant goads, heads of black buck, tortoise shells, peacock feathers, an easel that Vera had used twenty years before, Jim's school cricket bat, a bag of ship's bunting, a leather whip and tribal canoe paddles, it was to hear his wife's voice coming from the drawing-room. '. . . it's absolutely ridiculous, the wages they pay in

17

England. We take them on as raw girls of fifteen, lick them into some sort of shape as cook-generals, and then it's off with them. I never know from one day to the next if Bridie —' Her eyebrows lifted in would-be surprise. 'Have you only just come in, Henry? The coffee is half cold.'

'Ah, for goodness sake, woman . . .'

After several rounds of 'Hearts', he proposed that he see Jenny home.

'Oh no, Dodo. You — you mustn't bother.'

'Of course he must see you home,' Vera burst out hospitably. 'It's only just down the road.'

Vera studied her in surprise. Had there been a note of urgency? 'Why, Jenny, we wouldn't hear of your going home alone in the dark!'

Jenny glanced at Henry from under her lashes. It was heady, being a king's favourite.

Vera hobbled to the doorstep. Was the night really as balmy as Henry, who hadn't put on his overcoat, said it was? She watched them pass down the drive.

They walked a little apart. Perhaps Jenny wasn't finding it quite so easy to think of Dodo in isolation since Jim's taking up work at the office and Vera's fall. But — the night was powdered with stars. In the dusk, the half-seen trees and shrubs stood so still that they seemed to listen. Despite the rustle of his feet in a patch of leaves, there was a stillness too about Henry. He noticed her drifting towards him. Did she want him to take her arm? Loyalty to Vera demanded that he should not — A sharp expression entered his eyes. Loyalty to Vera? Jenny was almost a daughter, a *daughter!*

At her gate he paused by the bed that Jenny herself always tended, in daylight bright with the spears and subdued fires of early autumn flowers. 'I won't come in to see your mother this time. I ought to be getting back. Vera's ankle may be painful.'

'Yes.'

The muted light through the curtains of the sitting-room window caught the gold of her hair. Her night eyes were slumberous. As he was turnng away, he saw an appeal in them. He couldn't leave her thus without a kiss — a fatherly kiss. He put his strong engineer's hands on her shoulders. He bowed his lips to her petal cheek.

18

Suddenly she moved her head and her lips, soft as roses, enfolded his mouth. Her body melted into him. She felt the roughness of his face. Ah . . . At last she had given way to that insidious desire to be a proffered flower; a soft prey savaged by a beast. A beast? No, no. All she was doing was compromising between assertion and surrender by yielding to a god. Yielding? Dodo had always been in the position of a father (and only imperceptibly, if one closed one's eyes a little, changing into something else). She didn't have to worry about her beloved Vera; she was doing her no harm. With a sudden sigh she sold herself into the arms that now possessed her. The velvet star-embroidered cloak of the night wrapped them round.

She felt his dragon's breath on her cheek. His tweedy muscles coiled in aggression. As he bent forward, the light no longer fell on his face; he became a huge impersonal shape looming over her under the stars. His embrace seemed to change into a stifling of her, the big mouth and shaggy moustache and beard pressing on her face to become brutish. Afar-off daydream gods have romance without sex; they don't forget Vera. Revulsion and panic came together. Where had the father gone; whither the man of religion? With a stifled sound, she put her hands against his chest and pushed. He released her at once. She ran a few steps towards her door, then glanced back. The dark curtain-light once more fell on his face. His deep-set eyes gazed at her. Her walk became a slow pacing, her locks falling forward over her cheeks as she bowed her head.

He had been shocked to feel the desperation in the hands pushing him away. Was she being playful? He saw her glance back. Yes, that was it. She was merely being playful.

At her door she turned. In the midst of revulsion there had been excitement. Even if she had surrendered for a moment, it had been only a pleasant piece of play-acting that fulfilled a side of her nature without menacing the main part; there could not possibly, with Dodo, be involved any deep giving of herself. She studied the dignity of his grey-flecked hair, the steady eyes touched with uneasiness. She had insulted him. If she lost her position with him, it would serve her right. She smiled at him. Just before she closed the door behind her, she blew a kiss.

Henry strode away. Delightful and uncomfortable sensations jostled one another in his head. What had made her turn her lips like that? She had adopted him as a make-do father. Had she also adopted him as a make-do Jim? She was still very young and didn't really know herself.

Up in her room, Jenny took a cardboard box from a shelf. She removed the lid. A smile on her lips, she extracted the doll. It had been her favourite. How often in childhood she had dressed and undressed it, using the box as its cot! Suddenly she put it to her breast and so held it, swaying gently and crooning.

Chapter Two

A cat crouched on the top of one of the twin stone pillars. With the alert intensity of its kind, it followed with gold-flecked eyes the motion of the sleek limousine as it slid through the gateway. Henry Hampton, behind the steering-wheel, shifted on the upholstered seat. He was always a little uneasy in the presence of cats. They knew too much.

He observed with a pulse of excitement a head of light gold shoulder-length hair. The hair was partly covered by a violet kerchief to match the eyes. Charming! In nineteen thirty-five a lady of course would not dream of entering a church with her head uncovered, not even a lady who often teetered on the edge of rebellion. But an actual hat Jenny refused to wear, despite his promptings. That kiss she had given him full on the lips . . . It was all a little — a little irregular. He still didn't know quite what to make of it.

As a church-warden responsible, together with Canon Moss and the other church-wardens, for the building and grounds, Henry's brown eyes roved around. The grey-stoned family vaults, lining either side of the short drive, seemed well enough kept. The sexton had evidently washed their white marble tablets. The grass between the vaults had been clipped. The largest of them bore the word, HAMPTON. As he passed it, there seemed to reverberate to him, from its interior, ancestral murmurs — those murmurs that, along with his bible, guided him in all his thinking. He had a vision of the mother at whose silken knees he had learned of Jesus' love; and of the father with stern mutton-chop whiskers and sterner principles.

His car halted. Its silver radiator gleamed frostily at the lopsided back of Canon Moss's ancient grey Morris Cowley, like an aristocrat with his nose forced to within three feet of a tramp. Canon Moss himself stood before his church, his block of a form square in its long black cassock. His enormous expanse of chest and stomach heaved as he breathed. His hairy fingers were spread upon his cassock in the region of his shoulders. Despite his sixty-five years, he appeared to Henry to have recovered well from his recent heart attack.

'H-e-l-l-o Henry, Vera, Jim!' He sang out the greeting in the heavenly-trumpet tones that he sometimes employed in the pulpit.

No less solid, as though it had absorbed his prsonality after his having preached there for thirty years, stood the ancient stone fabric of St. Patrick's. No less square rose its tower. Even the bronze tones of the bell seemed an enlargement of Canon Moss's voice and a reinforcement of its message.

Henry, emerging from his car with his wife Vera and son Jim, after a nod to the Canon and the parishioners in general, applied himself to Jenny in particular. A paternal arm about her shoulders, he bent down from his great height. His beard pressed upon his neatly knotted tie. Despite his doubts about the regularity of that kiss, he looked round into her face. The man who had in his time ruled over sometimes unruly dockside workers in Karachi, was not the sort of man who permitted doubts to inhibit him for long. Doubt was not a path to getting his own way even when, as now, he preferred to leave exactly what that way was, indeterminate in his mind.

'How would you like to come for a drive this afternoon?' His tone was bantering. He turned to his wife. 'Vera, why ken't you be like Jenny and get a tan?'

Jenny was shyly avoiding his eye. Perhaps that kiss, in the form that it had taken at the last moment, had surprised her no less than him.

'Well, we'll see, we'll see,' he said, removing his arm.

He noticed that his son Jim was nibbling at his long forefinger. The boy's eyes were on his mother. Was he noticing the reddening of her cheekbones? Vera's cheekbones often seemed to redden when he, Henry, talked to young girls. He never could see any justification for it. After all, all that he was ever doing was ragging them. Young girls liked to be ragged. Sometimes he got the impression that Jim seemed to think that anybody over the age of forty was there solely to run the world for the young! Now the boy was looking at Jenny.

Was he noting, in her swaying back on her hips, a hint of languishmnent?

Jenny's mother, Mildred Byrne, tossed her head. She cast a coquettish glance at Henry from under the brim of a beflowered straw hat. This hat looked as if it had been painted with the same shiny black varnish as the bottoms of the boats down on the quay. 'Yes, Jenny, why don't you go for a drive?' Mildred noticed Henry's eye on her. 'Are you admiring my milkmaid complexion?' She gave her jolly laugh.

Milkmaid complexion! The woman was all piss and wind. (It was Henry's one Rabelaisianism, never uttered, naturally, in the presence of ladies.) More like high blood pressure from too much smoking.

He caught Jenny stealing a doubtful glance at his wife Vera. She wanted to go! Jim was frowning. What business was it of his son's? He had scarcely been aware of her existence for the past five years, three at Oxford, one learning printing in London, one studying art in Paris. Why should Jim care? On his mother's account? The breeze lifted and fell, shaking down a lock over Jenny's brow. She shook it back with a graceful toss of her head. Perhaps his son was thinking that she was no longer the gawky schoolgirl that he had left behind . . .

'Thank you, Dodo.'

Now Canon Moss was frowning! His heart condition, doubtless, still occasionally troubled him.

'What about Jim?' said Vera. 'I'm certain he'd like to go too.'

Jenny's mother Mildred looked sharply at Vera. Had there been a touch of animus against her daughter — one's other self, through whom one flirted with Henry? Perhaps not. Vera was fond of Jenny.

Henry began to bluster. 'Jim needs to put in some extra work if he's to get on in the office.' He couldn't ketch what all the fuss was about.

The boy's mouth had tightened. He pushed up on his forehead the black sombrero, a purchase in the boulevard Saint-Michel during his Paris art studies. 'Come off it, Dad! That's all baloney!'

Henry's lips twitched. 'I mean to say . . .'

'Perhaps,' interposed Mildred quickly, 'Jim prefers to work.'

Jim might be the ultimate prize, but in the mean time she set herself at all times to keep Henry happy. It wasn't her fault if his 'crush'

23

on her daughter might be putting Vera's nose out of joint. It wasn't her fault if Vera hadn't a milkmaid complexion and racehorse ankles. But she respected her social position. Mildred's own father wasn't — well . . . In that little shop in Cork selling apples to the children at so much each instead of by the pound. If only Dad would put 'Ltd.' after his name above the display window!

Vera ignored Mildred, who she knew cut no ice with her husband. 'Henry! You expect Jim to work on Sunday? You, the sabbatarian!'

'He doesn't mind shutting himself up in that studio of his on Sundays, painting, and neglecting his parents.'

Jim thrust his long thumbs into the pockets of his embroidered waistcoat. 'That's all my eye and Betty Martin! You know perfectly well — '

'Ah Henry, what nonsense!' intervened Vera quickly, laughing round at the company to save the family's face.

Canon Moss's head, with its cropped scant grey hair, turned on his bull neck as he surveyed the group. His face worked in a series of expressions of good-humoured pugnacity. He kept sucking in and shooting out his thick lips, while his mobile and aggressive jaw moved in and out like a piston.

After a glance at Vera's reddening cheekbones, he thrust out his tongue at Henry, only to snap it back into his mouth again. 'Don't you trouble, Hampton,' he trumpeted. He looked at the ledger under the latter's arm. There was a momentary gleam of apprehension. 'You've your accounts to do. I'll take out Jenny and Jim.' His baritone voice shot up unexpectedly into a high thin laugh. It was as though its owner had two voices.

His eyes were on Jenny's soft hands clasped about her prayer-book. High time that young lady was married off. Otherwise there might be a recurrence of what once before had brought her mother Mildren Byrne to him seeking his advice. He had called in Dr O'Grady and all had been well — for the time being. 'She's pretty, isn't she, Jim? I should grab her quickly. I think she's free at the moment.' He winked at Mildred.

Jim thrust his thumbs deeper into his waistcoat pockets. Grab her! He was damned if he would go where he wasn't wanted. But he managed a smile that might be interpreted as the company chose. 'Thanks, Padre.'

24

Padre! The folds and creases of Canon Moss's face shone; it was a good title. Something military about it. He threw back his vast shoulders and gave a little click with his heels, as though he remembered the time when, up to some thirteen years before, in 1922, he had been chaplain to the British forces then stationed in King William Fort. 'Good chap! Three o'clock sharp. Yankee waistcoat!' Again the high thin laugh.

Jim, knowing that his waistcoat, for all its unrestrained splendours, was of pure Irish design, grinned without comment. 'Yankee', in Canon Moss's mouth, meant anything new-fangled, not according to the good old ways.

Mildred Byrne's 'racehorse' ankles and small feet frisked plumply on the gravel. After all, Jim *was* the ultimate object of her hopes. Abruptly she ceased to frisk. His father was the owner of her house. He let it to her at a very low rent, for her daughter Jenny's sake she didn't doubt. Mildred wasn't getting any younger; she had to think of herself. And yet . . . If Jim wasn't forthcoming, Jenny, with her drive towards motherhood, might go and marry someone else. It was a subtle and sometimes bewildering game that had to be played.

'I mean to say, man —' Henry's voice was a growl. 'Er, Padre,' he amended quickly. His respect for Canon Moss's office was immense. But, his face still red, he half opened the account book. 'There's an item here that seems to me very irregular.'

The brazen throat of St Patrick's had just ceased to shake the air. The thin ring of the five-minute bell took its place.

'Must go and robe now.' The padre's short wide form was already retreating hastily towards the vestry. But he managed to wave a hairy paw in a gesture of cheerful Christian farewell.

Henry raised the ledger like a weapon. 'I'll see you in the vestry after the service.' Without waiting for his family, he marched into the church.

'Oh dear,' said Vera, 'I'm afraid the padre's in for a wigging.' She hastened after her husband.

There was a general drift of the parishioners towards the door. For a moment Jim found himself at Jenny's side. He glanced at her. Her blonde hair, save for the violet kerchief, fell untrammelled on her shoulders. Her wisp of a dress blew in the warm October morning breeze. Her long legs, usually bare, were clad in silk stockings. Why her distant behaviour since his return to Glenmorris? Was it resentment of his scant regard for her when she had idolised him as a little girl? Or was there someone else — of her own age, of course?

Out of the corner of her eye she regarded him. When, at nineteen, he had vanished to take up residence at Oxford, seldom coming back, so also had vanished her fourteen-year-old dreams. A correspondence she had tried to maintain had stifled under the blanket of a polite lack of enthusiasm from the other end. Her mind had become a temple glittering sombrely, with empty pedestal awaiting some new idol. Her feelings for Jim lay near-forgotten in the vaults beneath, in a white coffin, in a darkness filled with damp earth and bats' wings.

'Dad isn't too sensitive,' he remarked, 'as to what people think of him.'

'I don't agree. Sorry! He's *your* father. You have the right . . .'

'I just mean, he can't allow himself to be too sensitive. That would be a form of letting other people control him, and that he could never tolerate. On the contrary, his instinctive drive is to dominate others.'

'I admire men who can assert themselves.'

'Yes?' His smile carried no warmth. 'I was in India only as a small boy. But I remember him on one occasion, when his ship was tied up in Karachi Harbour and I was allowed on board, shouting on and on at his engine-room staff. I hated it. I longed for it to stop. As if he needs a counter-balance to this domination, his surrender to his upbringing is complete. It never occurs to him to question a word of it.'

Her resentment spilt over. 'I don't think you ought to talk about your father like this. He's the greatest man in this town. He hasn't got where he is on nothing.'

'No. No. He's got there on an immense capacity for work, for taking meticulous trouble. But his is a closed mind, a little iron circle of beliefs. Under stress, they could even destroy him, because he has no — no *give*.'

'You owe him plenty: Oxford, London, Paris.' She marched ahead of him into the church.

'I do indeed, I do indeed,' he said to her bristling back.

26

The service over, Henry, grasping the ledger, made his way grimly round to the vestry. 'I've checked over the parish accounts.'

'Oh, thanks very much, Hampton,' Canon Moss trumpeted unconvincingly.

'This item you've marked "Sundries",' — the padre's expression became that of a schoolboy caught stealing apples — 'I think that the Select Vestry will expect us to furnish them with a more exact description . . .'

'Mrs O'Grady, her little boy had no overcoat in which to go to school. His fingers were covered in chilblains.'

'That's all very well.' Henry barely kept the hectoring tone out of his voice. 'But there are proper channels through which to do such things. I mean to say . . .'

As the lecture proceeded, Canon Moss, who understood very well that Henry *was* the Select Vestry, turned aside and went through the motions of disrobing. He was too good a member of his democratic Church to deny the powerful controlling hand of the laiety. Besides, Henry was in the right. The Canon's little unauthorised hand-outs were as naive as they were debonaire. Henry's fierce monthly audits easily exposed his charitable pilferings and noble deceits.

'Er — look here, Padre, about Jenny —'

Canon Moss turned his massive form about, his small grey eyes resolute. 'Look forward to taking out Jim and her.' He thrust out his jaw, but no laugh followed to cancel the aggressiveness. 'Right that young people should go out together.'

'I was only going to take her out for a drive,' grumbled Henry.

The Canon prodded with a hairy finger one of the tassels of the red velvet-topped table on which lay the coins of the Collection. He watched it swinging to and fro. 'When I was a boy at my prep. school, I used to lisp. Didn't know I was lisping. The r's I pronounced as w's sounded like r's to me. It took the ridicule of the other boys to make me hear myself as I really was. From that moment I worked on my fault. At first I had to approach my r's at full charge, rolling them exaggeratedly. Later I managed them easily.'

Henry stared at him. Certainly the padre had been ill and wasn't getting any younger, but he surely wasn't beginning to ramble! 'What's this got to do with —'

27

Canon Moss's eyes met his. 'Such a thing as moral lisping.'

Henry swept the Collection into a steel tray and slid it into the safe. 'I must go. Vera and Jim are waiting.'

Outside the vestry door he paused. His jaw clenched. They, none of them, should exclude him from the world of youth. He would always be young. He was indestructible. But when he rejoined Vera and Jim all he said was, 'The padre's getting very odd.'

Chapter Three

A rook, alarmed by the passage of Henry's car down the hill, glanced its way upwards between two fir trees to alight high up in one of them, an elegant black flash in a green paradise. It was a day later, Monday, and Henry was returning to the office after lunch. Jenny Byrne observed the movement with exhilaration and disturbance. She was always exhilarated by beauty. She was disturbed because Dodo's granite profile beside her had not responded to her smiles all that morning.

Henry at that moment was, in fact, pointing out to himself that he couldn't blame her for the Sunday outing with his son Jim the day before. The outing had been engineered purely by Canon Moss. She had been more than willing to come out for a drive with himself. Of course, of course. As they entered the foyer of the Glenmorris Printing Company, he put his arm about her shoulders. She flashed a delighted smile at him.

Mrs O'Donovan, rising up from her bucket of slops, observed the gesture. 'The gentleman from Dublin is here, sir.'

Henry shone his smile at the waxed moustaches of the director of the woman's magazine, whom he found awaiting him in his office. 'Fifty thousand forty-page copies a month is rather more than we have taken on up to this. Fifty thousand! That's a tremendous circulation!'

The director laughed diffidently down his blue nose, his whiskers straying about his face. 'We can't hope, in this small country, to achieve the huge circulations that they do in London.'

Henry tapped his teeth with his pencil. 'It will mean installing a new machine. We like handling periodicals. Means steady work, month after month. Look here, while I'm going over this make-up, would you like my secretary Miss Byrne to show you the new extension?'

''Twould be very nice.'

He watched them depart. His brown eyes dimmed somewhat as he observed the director shooting lady-killer badinage at Jenny Byrne from under his moustache.

Henry quickly familiarised himself with the make-up, then made his way to the extension. The liberal supply of skylights in the tiled roof warmed the powerful dome of his head as he walked down the long single-storeyed building. It remained only for the new machines to be installed. He stood with Jenny watching the shiny black and chromium back of the director's car on its way to Dublin.

'More like August than October, Jenny!' The perfume of petals filled the still air. Smoke, too lazy to leave, sat on the chimneys. Hot sunflowers burned in a border. A bird, taking off from the water, shook a rainbow from its wings. He held up his face to the sunshine. The intense light picked out the strong structure of brow, cheekbone and jaw. The expression of relaxation sat oddly on features usually tense with conscientiousness and ambition.

'It seems a shame, Dodo.'

He looked at her closely. 'What?'

'To have to go back to the office.'

A red-sailed dinghy was peacocking about the harbour. A speed-boat, gathering pace, raised its nose to the sky.

He caught his breath. He glanced at her breasts and long legs. Was she inviting him . . . No, of course not. He plunged his hand into the pocket of his tweed jacket. There was the rustle of paper. He popped a boiled sweet into his mouth. From his waistcoat pocket he drew the gold watch which he had inherited from his father — the watch that drove him on. Flat on its back, it glinted in the sunlight in the hollow of his great palm. 'Tch! Only three o'clock! Three more hours before the office closes!' But it wasn't every day that one brought off a deal like that just concluded. 'Those gulls are fishing.' He glanced across the harbour at a flurry of white wings rising, wheeling, and falling like stones. 'What do you say to seeing if we can pick up a mackerel?'

Her deep violet eyes regarded him. Mackerel in Glenmorris Harbour in October!

Henry had the grace to twitch his moustache. 'If it isn't too late in the year. The fishermen catch the odd one.' He cocked his eye on her sharply, his expression become severely practical. 'That is, if you can spare the time.'

A sudden little warm breeze lifted the golden fringe of hair that fell on her forehead, with its slight autumn tan. She examined the dimpled backs of her hands. 'It's for you to say whether or not I can spare the time.'

He could have wished that she had been more helpful. He led their forward movement out of the doorway. As he did so, he glanced upwards at a window in the front of the great red-brick building, just above the board running along its length and bearing in white letters the legend 'Glenmorris Printing Company'. He lowered his voice. 'Better let Jim suppose that we're still with the publisher.' He didn't attempt to explain why.

She hesitated. 'Yes.'

The tide was low, and the side of the quay rose high above them as Henry's great form bent to the oars. Weeds and limpets clung to the crevices in the slaty stone. Up to high-water mark the stone was dark. Thereafter it became light grey. For as long as possible he used the height of the quay to mask the boat from his son's office window. But the cat basking on its edge, not the same cat that had observed his approach to the church, not even a relation of that cat, but with the same gold-flecked eyes, was taking notes of all his movements.

'Oh look at Canon Moss's yacht!' said Jenny. 'The burgee is still flying. He's always forgetting to haul it down. I'm his crew; shouldn't we row over?'

Henry glanced back above her head to the office window. 'Better not do it now.' You'd almost suppose the foolish child was having second thoughts! Some people could never relax. 'We have to be back sharp for dinner at seven.'

As the Glenmorris Printing Company dropped astern, so did Henry feel the shackles of what society expected of him as husband to Vera, father to Jim, head of an old family, pillar of the church, leader of the business community, falling from the limbs of his spirit. He wouldn't have wished to be without them. They were the complement of the whole man. But the aggregate burden of them, as life had added first one, then another, took toll of his freedom. While he had the weight on him he seldom noticed it, because he didn't question its right to be there. But now that he had laid it down for a sunlit hour, his spirits soared like the white wings piercing up into the blue ahead. He heard old sounds with a new delight — the children reciting in chorus some lesson in the convent school, the chug of a trawler's engine at the pier-head, the deep sigh of a siren in the outer harbour, the complaint of a gull.

A boat drove past them, propelled by a second-hand motor-car engine which had been installed in a space in her centre separated off by two crudely made wooden partitions. The rest of the unseaworthy old hulk, both bow and stern, was filled to the gunwale with a cargo of sand culled from some beach near the mouth of the harbour. A shabby young fellow in a cloth cap, crouching on top of the sand, steered her by a wooden tiller. His cargo would be bought by the nuns, being found excellent for the growing of carrots.

'Have you left any of the beach behind?' shouted Henry, chaffing him.

The fellow gave back a meaningless grin.

'He's not right in the head, you know,' murmured Jenny.

They reached the spot where the gulls had been fishing. She made no move to put out a line, nor did Henry suggest that she should. She half lay back against the stern, the fingers of one hand trailing in the autumn-warm water. Though her lashes were lowered, he was aware that her eyes were on his fists upon the oar handles. Perhaps she was savouring the power behind each forward surge of the boat. He increased the force of his stroke. Swans in their path took off, their wings whipping the heavy air. A flight of wild geese on their winter migration screamed by overhead, tearing the sky apart.

Perhaps she in her turn was conscious of her rounded dimpled knees slightly apart, and of his gaze on them. At her feet was the can which accompanied Henry on all fishing expeditions. Holding the caught fish with his left hand and inserting the first and second fingers of his right into its gills, he would take it over the side of the boat as a precaution against the squirt of faeces and blood to follow. The fish would give a convulsive shudder as its head was forced back to the point at which the backbone broke. 'Why do you do that, Dodo?' Jenny as a little girl had screwed up her eyes. Henry had washed the bloodstained corpse in the sea before throwing it into the tin. 'My father taught me it was cruel to allow them to stifle slowly.' He was one of the few fishermen in Glenmorris who didn't leave them to flounder out their lives in the bottom of the boat. But now it was four o'clock; there yet remained an hour and a half before the sun would set behind the residences of Upper Glenmorris. Its glory put a bar of gold across the harbour, and a miniature one across the burnished hair that framed Jenny's face.

The boat began to rise and fall to the swell of the outer harbour. A porpoise rolled across its breadth like a rubber Catherine Wheel, showering sparklets of water off its sleek hide.

'What a lovely little beach, Dodo! I've seen that wood from the Fort. I've always wanted to explore it.'

They landed.

'Be careful, Jenny! There's a kink in the path here. I've suggested to the Urban District Council that it should be straightened. People like to come here on a Sunday.'

She laughed. 'You *are* funny, Dodo!'

As though woken from a dream, he started. 'What'd that?'

'The way you want everything straight. D'you remember that time you were designing the cover of *The Hotel & Boarding-house Register*?'

Henry's high forehead reddened. He knew well enough what she had been thinking; that his design was dry and technical. Just because he would never draw freehand! Well, he had been a ship's engineer and he had no intention of apologising for lines drawn hard and uncompromising. Truly Henry's moral evasions did not extend into his draughtsmanship! He had looked at her. When other children, growing up, had abandoned their drawing and water- colouring, Jenny had persisted.

'D'you think it would be better to put the title a little more to the left?' she had said.

'But that would be off centre. I should have thought that the geometrical centre was the right place for it. The whole thing is based on a rectangle. It would put a — a kink in the design.'

She had smiled. 'Geometry's all right, but then instinct has to take over.'

He shook aside the memory. It was destroying the daydream in which he wished to immerse himself. He took her hand — purely because kinks might cause young ladies to stumble. As they ascended the slope, there lay about them furze and fern, and the glass floor

33

of the sea and the roof of the sky extending to the horizon. Henry gradually ceased to have any plans. He knew only that he was young again and wanted to wander on and on, out of the reach of his home Karachi House, of the Glenmorris Printing Company, of the Church Select Vestry, of the Urban District Council, of the ticking of his watch, into a timeless sunset of yellow scented autumn.

Her hand in his was warm and soft. Tenderness swelled in him. He transferred his arm to her waist. With a sudden rough little movement he drew her against him. She half closed her eyes and sighed; he wanted to hurt her! Ah . . . He felt the silk of her hair as she nestled her head on his shoulder. He laid his cheek against her hair. So he led her, his nostrils filled with the faint scent of sun-dried ferns, towards the sound of lazy water and the velvet scolding of pigeons.

The rivulet in the wood, a murmurous thunder, threw green coils over and round cool boulders. It slid with jewelled eyes into the recesses of overhanging boughs. They scrambled across shiny stones to an islet in a sun-flecked eddy. Seated a short distance from her, he watched her bathe her feet, his senses entranced by the voice of the brook. It seemed to him that in those brown limbs dipping into green coolness lay all the youth of the world; youth that brushes past like a moth's wing, as had his own . . .

His thoughts drifted away into the what-might-have-been. But always he watched those limbs. Time floated by on powder-yellow cloudlets.

Darts driven into his neck and scalp brought him back to the present. He rubbed at the minute goads. Gnats and midges were beginning to appear, bright sparks sailing in the withdrawing sun. Purple air blew over the evening sea.

'Jenny, it's getting late.'

She moved her naked legs up and down in the water. Doubtless his eyes on her were setting in action the ancient impulse to attract.

'Jenny, I think we ought to be making our way back to the boat.'

The stream drowned his voice.

Obliged to move nearer, he touched her shoulder. Feeling its lissomness, he drew in his breath. He passed his palm again and again over her back, the wool of her cardigan between his hand and the softness of the flesh. He felt no surprise at what he was doing. The islet of ferns had become the whole of the universe; he was suspended in a magic moment cut off from all the rest of time. She half turned towards him, drawing her feet out of the water. He pressed her down across his lap, her soft breasts beneath his chest, until her shoulders were on the ground. She had closed her eyes. If it occurred even now to Henry that, in the great composition of life (doubtless based on a moral rectangle), what he was doing was distinctly off centre, yet he moved to his destruction. She also, it seemed, was too far gone to be heedful of consequences. So the sighing and the panting of the machinery of love moved on as inexorably as the belts clacking over the pulleys in the Glenmorris Printing Company.

Suddenly she felt his full weight. The sensation, and that of his hands pulling away her clothing and feeling for her body, but fulfilled, for a moment, the entrancement of being a prey savaged by an animal. But then came the further sensation of being penetrated at a point where desire quickly gave way to a feeling of outrage. Her position beneath him was *not* one of abandonment; it was one of inferiority! There came a sharp pain. It radiated throughout her whole body. She began to push him. That would make him go away, as it had before at her gate. But rather only he seemed to come on. She was engaged in a full-scale struggle with someone who was no longer Dodo, but a stranger. She beat at his shoulders with her fists. 'Leave me alone, leave me alone.'

He seemed to go limp. He lay upon her a huge inert weight, breathing heavily. He was going from her. He rolled over on to his side, fumbling at his clothes. She rose, arranging her own with trembling fingers. They stood up.

He looked at her from under his shaggy brows. He put his hand on her shoulder. 'There's nothing to worry about —'

She shuddered away. 'Don't touch me!'

His brown eyes were urgent. 'Jenny, I assure you you don't have to be afraid that —'

'Afraid! You just disgust me.'

She walked rapidly towards the boat. So this was the reality towards which the reverie of courtship led! This was the man on whom her eyes had rested in the church as he had read the lessons!

The top of the lectern was in the guise of an eagle, whose stretched wings supported the massive bible. The eagle stood poised upon a golden ball, its fiery beak and slanting eyes turned upon the people, a stream of coloured sunshine, travelling through stained glass and arches, striking fire from its brass feathers. Poised behind the book had stood Dodo, his powerful handsome features urgent in the stained light, his eyes turned upon the congregation.

Perhaps Henry, as with twitching lips he stepped into the boat after Jenny, was reflecting that, in the relatively straight path of his way through life, here was a kink that not even the Glenmorris Urban District Council could straighten out. Had she been leading him on? Or had she merely been basking in his admiration? Had he misread the signals? She was still very young and didn't really know herself, and that made it all very confusing.

They moved urgently through the blackening water. The sun had set an hour since. The indigo sky was pierced by early stars. A flash of phosphorescence marked the passage of the oar blades as Henry rowed with long strokes. Half an hour in which to get back to the quay, to make fast, and to drive home for dinner!

The intense effort had a calming effect on his racing brain. Admittedly he had lost his head and gone too far. But, as he pointed out to himself, a man was no less a Christian because he sometimes fell. There were others whose lives came far below his. He avoided her eyes. He gazed past her form, sitting rigid in the stern, as though he wished to pick out some detail in the darkening line of the shore. Just a deep affection for a girl which had turned into . . . Quite outside his control. A sort of nervous breakdown, no doubt. He had been overworking recently. He must keep away from her in the the future, of course. He would go and see Dr O'Grady. It had been a shock, to feel her contempt. Would — would she tell . . . Soon the deepening dusk came to his aid, and put its saving mask over their features.

He turned his head. A light had appeared on his port bow. It was the leading boat of a part of the Glenmorris fishing fleet, sadly shrunken in this year of 1935, proceeding a full hour and a half earlier than usual out to sea. The long black boat slid through the ghost-grey twilight, two men rowing the heavy oars on the lea side, one rowing an oar on the windward. The fourth member of the crew stood in the stern, partly steering, partly sculling, with another oar. Amidships was an iron rod, attached upright to the side of the boat. The rod ended in two prongs holding a lantern between them to give light to the night's labour. Behind this boat there followed another, also bearing a lantern, and then another, and another. He counted nine in all. They dropped away astern, as he had seen them go many a time of a winter's evening, a sad little carnival, rowing out to sea upon their lonely business, to return with their catch in the bitter early morning hours.

As Jenny began to recognise Dodo again, so doubtless once more, as had happened when the curtained light had fallen on his face at her gate, did the violent stranger recede. Perhaps for the second time she was learning, as she watched him rowing there so disturbed, that the body of the powerful beast, man, was inhabited and inhibited by a brain as vulnerable as her own. If she had not allowed things to proceed so far, she could have pushed him away once again. Yes, until she had panicked at the last moment, she had taken her full part in the matter . . . After all Dodo, despite everything, was reverent towards women. 'Look out! The quay!'

He glanced over his shoulder. Only ten yards separated the bow from a looming shape. He thrust in his right blade, holding water with all his strength. The boat swung round parallel to the quay. Something tickled his face. He rubbed at the spot. It was sweat. He pulled at his cuffs to ease the cling of his shirt sleeves.

The boat moored, they stood by the empty mine case at the foot of the street lamp, which picked out the slipway leading up to the quay. The mine case, relic of the War, lay there emptied of its explosives, like a denizen of the deeper waters stranded on the shore. Hollow, rusty brown, it rose to Henry's chest. He was aware that they were just below Jim's attic studio in the building next to the printing works. There was no light in the window. The boy had doubtless discovered from the junior partner Mr Sparrow, a man with a sharp nose and a bird-like ability to peck up a bargain, that they had not returned from their attendance on the director. He could imagine the boy's lithe stride to the car parked on the pier-head. He could see the query in the blue eyes, so like Vera's, when his father did not arrive to drive him to dinner. Henry's square fingers rubbed at his bottom; doubtless, in the course of his hectic row, the thwart had caused an abrasion. Then the boy had certainly made his way to that so-called studio of his to collect his bicycle. Cycling along the quay, he would notice that the boat was not at her moorings. What would he think? The boy had the mercilessness of twenty-four; he didn't allow his judgments to be clouded by charity . . .

Henry glanced from under shaggy brows at the tapered fingers curved uneasily over the edge of the hole at the top of the case. He thought that she had softened a little towards him; she would not tell. 'It's all right. It will be all right,' he said to the mine. It wasn't as if he'd lost his head completely. He knew how to manage these things. Well — almost certainly.

Her eyes under their golden fringe told him that he had guessed her thought aright. She smiled wistfully. Perhaps she too had been shocked that she had spoken to him so.

He held his gold watch up to the street light. 'Tch, tch! Ten to seven!'

The first thing that he noticed at Karachi House was his son's black sombrero hanging on the hall-stand. He entered the drawing-room, ushering in Jenny before him. Vera was warming her hands at the fire.

'Sorry we're late.' His eyes didn't quite meet hers. 'We've been celebrating the award of a very valuable contract.'

'Have you only just arrived, Henry?' Considering that Vera was talking to one of her 'boys', the reproving expression on her lips was surprisingly severe, the smile that she endeavoured to maintain on them at such a time unusually faint. Jim had told her that the boat was missing from its moorings. Her surprise had sharpened into anxiety as the quarter-hours had chimed on the grandfather clock in the hall. And now to find that Henry had merely been gadding about!

'Celebrating!' Jim had just strolled into the room. 'Wish I could have joined in the celebration. With a second oarsman, you could have gone twice as fast and twice as far.'

'Judging from their lateness,' objected Vera illogically, 'I think they went far enough.'

Henry fixed his gaze on the chandelier. 'Jenny and I were seeing off the director. We did it on the sput of the moment.'

Jim considered his mother. Surely even her need to believe in her family and closest friends couldn't disguise from her that this was all my eye and Betty Martin. He couldn't tell, he couldn't tell . . . Of her sensibilities he could have no doubt; it was from her that he had inherited his own. But neither could he doubt her charity.

Henry drew back a corner of a curtain. Somewhere out in the twinkling darkness were the grove, and the fishermen upon their business. His son, he felt sure, was thinking that he had been the architect of the outing; that Jenny could have only a hero-worshipping attachment to a man so much older. It was just as well.

Over the dining-room table he looked at his wife. He would never let her down again. Never. He rose abruptly. One seemed to notice less the strong bone structure of his face, and more its fleshiness; less the straightness of his back, and more his moustache and beard ever shrinking as he removed with his scissors the increasing number of grey hairs. He opened a window.

'Aren't you going to finish your soup?' enquired Vera. 'Don't tell me Bridie has again put too much salt in it! I'd get rid of her, only servants are so hard to come by. Not that she won't be taking off for England and its higher wages one of these days!'

'The Masterman siren buoy is very quiet. Ken't be much of a sea running,' he muttered to the curtain.

After the electric blaze in the dining-room, all seemed dark. As his eyes adjusted to the quieter light, he began to see the starlit lawn. The light from behind him caught the flowers in the bed under the window. A white butterfly rested on one of them. He leaned out and touched it. It was dead and dropped to the ground.

He made it Jim's task to see Jenny home. They had hardly set off, when she was back again for her handbag. He found it for her in the hall.

'Was it really so bad, Dodo?'

He glanced at her sharply. 'What?' He couldn't ketch her meaning.

'Can anything so painful be bad?'

His lip twitched severely. 'It was — highly irregular.' From where did the child get this indifference to principle? Her mother Mildred was conventional enough. Perhaps from her great-aunt Nellie, who had eloped with a Roman Catholic butcher to Waterford, of all places.

'Yes.' She left, walking slowly, her head bowed.

At the bottom step she paused and looked at him. The wistfulness in her troubled face made his heart turn over, and haunted him afterwards. She was gone in the dusk to rejoin Jim. He awaited her on the drive, the headlamp of his bicycle switched on.

Henry joined Vera in the bedroom.

'I'm glad, darling,' she said, 'that you took a bit of the afternoon off. Poor old boy! You always have your nose to the grindstone.'

Really, she had behaved earlier in the evening as though she had been jealous of Jenny! Jenny, at this very moment being seen home by Jim! Jenny, virtually Henry's daughter! That's what Henry had always wanted, a daughter as well as a son. Her mood, as ever on this theme, became defensive. Why should people always suppose that a lack of fertility was the woman's? It could be Henry's.

As he tied the cords of his pyjama trousers, he glanced at the silver-backed brush, her initials on it, passing and repassing up the nape of her fine neck and over her thick brown hair. The years had been able to make little impact in the face of her simple and healthy life. She was as beautiful as ever. Why should she suspect him? She naturally expected fidelity because of his religion and hers. But she had made it hard for him . . . Abruptly he crossed the room. He put his hands on her shoulders and kissed her cheek.

Her quick smile turned to concern. There was a stream of moisture down the hard face. 'Are you feeling well, old boy? You didn't allow yourself to get a chill after being overheated from rowing?' In their days in Karachi in the then Indian province of Sind, from which the shipping company had operated, the theory was that Henry could stand the heat of the climate and of the engine-room because of the profuseness with which he perspired. But as Vera had seldom been able to persuade him, his task accomplished, to put on his jacket again, he had caught more than one chill and she had had to nurse him through the ensuing fever.

'Ah, for goodness sake, woman . . .' But the grumble was unconvincing.

He turned away to put on his dressing-gown. Picking up his toothbrush, he went out.

Her lips pouted thoughtfully. From a wall cabinet she extracted a bottle of aspirins. She placed them with a glass of water on the table between the beds. She closed her lids on blue eyes still troubled.

Henry put on the landing light. Against the dark wood of the door, his face appeared even more pallid. He placed his palm against the wardrobe in which the blankets were kept. Gripping the bannisters, he got himself down towards the bathroom. He rested on the soiled-linen chest that stood on the half-way landing.

There, down below in the great hall, was Vera's folding easel and stool, bringing back memories of their early married days before she had given up her sketching. Did she not want romance too? Where lay her dreams? A deep affection for her family and friends seemed to suffice. There were the spears and the tortoise shell and the peacock feathers and the canoe paddles garnered by his father on a world cruise. As he looked at them, he had a vision of a tall figure with stern mutton-chop whiskers, beloved and revered, and of his own childhood. There, in the umbrella-stand, stood Jim's school cricket bat; Jim, his son, before whom he should have stood as a pillar. Indeed, he should so have stood before Jenny too.

The church bell began to shake the sad evening air. Moral lisping . . . He had committed adultery! He hadn't just lost his head. It wasn't a case of a man's sometimes slipping from his ideals. There was no nervous breakdown. What would have been Jim's word for that? Baloney! He had committed adultery against Vera, against Jenny, against her mother, against his son, against his own father and mother — against God. Adultery, adultery, adultery . . .

He put his head in his hands. The edifice, slowly and unconsciously built up through the years to allow the vigorous body to live in partnership with the puritan mind, had thrust its foundations deep. The mighty fabric cracked and split apart unwillingly, and only with immense pain.

'O God have mercy upon me, for I am a great sinner.'

Chapter Four

Jim Hampton stood at his office window. The early November frost had edged the tops of the quay and slips, and the gunwales of the long black fishing-boats, with needle-sharp outlines of silver-white. The sun, in a last struggle to assert itself, bathed a hill and a huddle of cottages in a welter of watery saffron. A tree raised its bare arms, black tracery against a patch of dark blue sky.

He sat down. His lean hand, its autumn tan all but faded, reached out for a switch. His work was illuminated from below through the glass top of the desk. He pulled on his cheroot and propelled a fragrant blue ring at his tracing.

He heard the intercom buzz in Jenny's office. She picked up her pencil and pad and, after a tap on his door, crossed his office. His father opened his door to her. Jim watched him stand courteously aside to allow her to pass. What, no arm about her shoulders! Now why? And since when? Since several weeks, perhaps a month. A month . . . What had happened a month ago? Nothing of any significance: letters dictated in his father's office; visits to Karachi House, like on the occasion after his father had taken her out for a row; conversations outside the church — a bunch of red roses, still fresh, quietly consigned to her wastepaper basket when she didn't know that his eye was on her.

The sound of the hooter for the end of the day's work arose. He slipped on his overcoat. Yes, that was it! His father's demeanour had altered *after the outing in the boat.*

Down in the foyer Mrs O'Donovan the cleaner, the steel-grey coils of her hair seemingly ready to snap on to any piece of evidence, noted that it was not Mr Hampton who was seeing Miss Jenny out, his arm about her waist. It was Mr Jim, with Mr Hampton going on ahead. Think o' that, now! 'Good night, sir.'

Henry paused at the car. 'Jenny, I wonder if you'd mind getting in at the back.' He pulled open the door. 'Jim, would you sit beside me. There are some church affairs I want to discuss with you.'

His son averted his eyes to a green and orange cascade of nasturtiums, flowering late in a freak sunny nook, pouring over a whitewashed wall. 'Not my line.'

Henry, whose moustache had begun to twitch, let in the clutch and the car moved along the quay. Earlier in the day, after reading over the lessons for next Sunday, he had turned to Leviticus. 'Do not cause thy daughter to be a whore.' The words of the plain-speaking Mosaic code had burned into his brain.

Up the short drive, boys with glee and Canon Moss's permission were collecting conkers. By the rectory itself, Canon Moss bent over a shallow Victorian hip-bath rescued out of his attic. His light was an electric bulb brought out on the end of a flex through the kitchen window. Jenny had remained in the car.

'Hello, you two!' He scraped with a shovel at the contents of the tub. 'Just mixing four parts of gravel to two of sand to one of cement.'

Henry surveyed the surroundings. Everywhere was, so to speak, concrete evidence of the Canon's industry — concrete trellises, concrete steps, concrete drains. It was said of Augustus Caesar that he found Rome brick and left her marble. Perhaps of the padre it would be said that he found the rectory brick and left it concrete.

Canon Moss straighted up. His eyes fell on Jim's orange waistcoat. 'Yankee!'

'I'd just like a word with you if I may.' Henry had wanted his son at his side to prevent any too deep probing by the Canon.

The latter, after a glance from under his wild eyebrows, thrust his spade upright into the mixture. He produced his pipe and placed it in the convenient space formed by the missing tooth in the lower right-hand side of his jaw. Clenching it there, he extracted flakes of tobacco from his pouch. 'Fire away, Hampton.'

'I think I should give up reading the lessons on Sunday.' Out of the corner of his eye, Henry caught Jim's movement of surprise.

Canon Moss appeared to be absorbed in grinding up the flakes of tobacco, using the top of the middle finger of his right hand as the pestle in the mortar of the cupped palm of his left. A match to the bowl, he puffed the pipe alight.

Henry studied these operations. Bad for the padre's heart. A little wooden thing sucking out his life. 'I think I should give up my church offices altogether. I'm not as young as I was. I'd be glad to help in the background; the auditing and so forth.'

The padre removed his pipe. 'Not as young! You're younger than you ever were.'

Henry responded with a faint smile in which was something of affection. 'I'm not as fit as I was.'

The padre's scrutiny became closer. The robust Henry was certainly pale. He was a man suffering loss of health — but was it of the body? He regarded the bowl of his pipe. 'Can I help in any way, Hampton?'

'I shall be all right.'

'You've been for many years the leading figure in our parish. Cause a lot of surprise.'

Henry had already thought of that. The well-meaning condolences of the parishioners would in themselves constitute a false position, but one that would pass. As far as Jenny was concerned, his small anxiety had all but vanished with the passing of a month. Yes, yes, he had been perfectly right when he told her that the chances of a pregnancy following a single — event — were almost nil. Of course he had been right.

'Stay on just for the moment. Give me time to look for another man. Need the help. Not up to what I used to be.'

Henry, smiling kindly, gave his sharp double nod. 'I appreciate that.' He turned to his son. 'Would you consider taking it on?'

'I'm not the man for the job, Dad.'

The Canon grinned. 'We need young blood. Even some of your Yankee ideas!'

'My Yankee ideas include agnosticism, if not atheism, Padre.'

'Guessed that might be the reason. But I wonder if you have really considered —'

Jim nodded. 'I've been listening to you chaps since I was taken off the pap.' He softened it with a smile. 'I know all your arguments by heart. But in spite of your teleological reasonings and the rest of them — and mighty unconvincing they are! — you really make your final stand on faith.'

44

The Canon thrust out his jaw. 'In science there's plenty of reliance on faith.'

'But *degree* matters. Religion has for me nothing like the mental discipline of the scientist in keeping an open mind, in conducting research and following it wherever it may lead, in considering closely the reliability of his own mind — and that of others.'

'Down the centuries religion has kept its hold on millions.'

'All sorts of things have kept their hold on millions, including the most palpable rubbish. People always want something easily and now. The Church more or less offers them instant truth. But truth has to be sweated for and waited for.'

'The Church conducts plenty of research into biblical events,' said the padre with unwonted heat.

Jim thrust his thumbs sharply into his waistcoat pockets. 'And goes all cock-a-hoop when someone shows there's a basis of truth to the Flood or the fall of the walls of Jericho. What on earth of any consequence is that supposed to prove? Since when did peasant tales ever not arise out of something that happened, embroidered out of recognition?'

'Well, Jim,' said the padre cooling down, 'we could be at this all night, and I can see that your father has worries. We must argue it out another time.'

Henry, whose realm was not speculation, had been listening to his son with disapproval and pride. The boy was talking nonsense of course and he would grow out of it, but it was quite impressive sounding nonsense.

When they parted ten minutes later they had settled on Dr O'Grady, or so Henry supposed. Or had the padre perhaps resolved on delaying tactics designed to secure Henry himself? Jim, looking back, reflected that, what with mixing concrete and smoking the battered pipe that had already injured his heart, the good Canon would undoubtedly kill himself. But in the meantime he would be happy in the prospect of meeting, in a Lutheran paradise, his Lord God, who would unquestionably prove to be an adherent to the Reformed Faith.

That evening, as always since his childhood, Henry knelt down at his bedside to pray. Earlier, Vera had done the same at hers. Now in bed, she was reading her bible. As always over the past month, he prayed for forgiveness; and that, if it were God's will, his deed should not bring unhappiness, even disaster, on those he had wronged.

At first his supplications had absorbed his whole being. But, as the days passed, he had ever more found them growing less real. Was he failing to reach God? Why should God forgive the enormity of his act, his gross transgression against his laws, on the head of a few mumbled words? How could he reach God again? Would he ever reach him again?

After kissing Vera on the cheek, he got into bed and opened his bible at random. He found himself reading the words, 'Then shall the King say unto them on his right hand, Come, ye blessed of my Father, inherit the kingdom prepared for you from the foundation of the world: For I was an hungred, and ye gave me meat: I was thirsty, and ye gave me drink: I was a stranger, and ye took me in: Naked, and ye clothed me: I was sick, and ye visited me: I was in prison, and ye came unto me. Then shall the righteous answer him, saying, Lord, when saw we thee an hungred, and fed thee? or thirsty, and gave thee drink? When saw we thee a stranger, and took thee in? or naked, and clothed thee? Or when saw we thee sick, or in prison, and came unto thee? And the King shall answer and say unto them, Verily I say unto you, Inasmuch as ye have done it unto one of the least of these my brethren, ye have done it unto me.'

Yes, when words grew stale, that was how to pray, to reach God. Not by talking, but by doing. By serving his brethren. Service never grew stale, never weakened, no, not over a lifetime. He must forget himself entirely. If confession were the best way to serve *others* (not himself), then he must confess. If not to put the cat among the pigeons was the best way to serve *others* (not himself), then he must continue to hold his tongue. And anything he did to make amends must be done unobtrusively. Not as the Pharisees; no public show. But how could he best serve Jenny, whom he had wronged perhaps the most? Or Vera, his wife, whom he had wronged scarcely less? Or Jenny's mother, Mildred? Or Jim? Or Canon Moss?

As far as public show was concerned, Canon Moss presented the greatest difficulty. The padre *needed* him, or at least wanted him, as a church warden, vestryman, reader of the Lessons, sidesman with others taking up the Collection. But each time he walked up to the lectern to read, or made his way down the aisle passing the collecting bag along the pews, he felt himself to be making the statement, 'I am, in a certain measure, a leader in this act of worship.' More, he felt himself to be saying, 'I am *worthy* so to lead.' That could not go on. He must press resolutely for Dr O'Grady to take over.

Background work like the auditing or, as an engineer, keeping an eye on the condition of the fabric of the church, that he could continue. If the sexton were ill or otherwise away, he could even take his place in mowing the churchyard grass or cleaning the monuments, provided that it was done late in the evening when no one was about. Should the padre come to notice, he could make his confession to him. It would go no further of course; bring no unhappiness to others. Over an extended period, one by one, he could withdraw from the Urban District Council, from the Glenmorris Printing Company handing over to Jim, finally from the neighbourhood, giving Vera a Legal Separation. Divorce was against their convictions, not that there *was* any divorce in Ireland. Jim would look after his mother and be a worthy head of the family.

He fell asleep more peacefully than he had for many a night.

Henry was as pale as Jenny.

'Are you sure?' It was the third time that he had asked the question since she had been shown into the drawing-room by Bridie the cook-general.

It was a month later, in the first week of December. A white town clung to the hillside. The sky, heavy with clouds, sat on the roof tops. Down in the harbour a bullying wind was knocking a lone yacht about. Earlier, the pale gold ball of the sun had sunk below a dark grey horizon, two last shafts of light striking a white field above King William Fort.

The firelight flickering over Jenny's young features seemed to Henry to lend them no warmth.

'I was sick.' Her fingers twisted and untwisted the handkerchief on her lap, the backs of her hands dimpling.

'My dear child, where? When?'

'In the scullery. The smell from the scrap bucket.'

He put in quickly, 'Did your mother see?'

She shook her head.

'Look — look here, are you sure it wasn't just something you ate?'

'I've been eating food, as usual.'

The sarcasm shook him as nothing else. The once adoring Jenny sarcastic to her Dodo! Not that it was 'Dodo' any more. Oh, the child had too much sensibility to change to 'Mr Hampton'. It was just — nothing. Of course he had withdrawn himself from her as far as possible long ago. She must have sensed that his hypocrisy was all gone; that the garden down which they had been wandering ended in a wall.

But there was an undertone of protest as he said, 'A bad smell *does* sometimes make people sick.'

'If I've had a tunny upset, it hasn't left me feeling on the edge of being sick every morning. I *know* the symptoms of pregnancy.'

He looked at her sharply. There had been so much vehemence! Gave him the impression that she was rejecting his suggestion not so much because she thought it wrong, as because there was something already in her mind that made her determined to reject it.

'Have you missed — I mean to say, have you missed . . .'

'Yes.'

'Look here, it may not be as you think. It's most unlikely that a single occasion —'

'Aren't you going to help me then?'

Her features, half turned away from him and the firelight, looked different. The chair creaked as his massive form leant forward. She was silently weeping. Jenny, the lissom Diana of fields and woods, weeping!

In a moment he was down beside her, a hand on her arm. 'Of course I'm going to help you, Jenny. That's my job. That's what I'm here for. If I did everything I could for you, in my prayers, with my advice, with my money, it wouldn't be half enough.' Massive or not, his whole body trembled in the vehemence with which he spoke. He withdrew his hand to rest his cheek on it, his elbow on his knee. The room darkened and swayed.

Jenny's eyes were on the facsimile of the fire winking in the shine of sweat on Henry's brow. She put her hands over her face. A sob burst through them. 'What am I to do?'

He gripped her knee. 'Jenny, Vera's only just outside in the greenhouse. She'll be back any minute.' What a fool he had been! His lovely marriage! Yes, in spite of a want left unsatisfied, a lovely marriage. He spoke slowly. 'I'm prepared to let Vera know of my appalling conduct, but I don't know how to do this without —'

Abruptly she ceased dabbing at her eyes with her handkerchief. 'No, no, no. I couldn't face her.'

'The whole responsibility was mine —'

'No. I took my full part.' In the kiss at her gate, on the islet of ferns, always there had been excitement. Coitus had been painful. But there was a change in her body; next time it would be different. He had been a tidal wave that had taken her up and hurled her on to a strange new shore.

'Jenny, in the beginning you wanted the expedition, yes. But by the time we reached the padre's yacht, with its burgee still flying, you were very much having second thoughts. It was only I that pushed you on. You are so much younger. I was almost in the place of your father. You trusted me.'

She shook her head. 'I'm nineteen. I would have known at *fifteen* that it was wrong.'

'Well . . . I'll send you up to Dublin to see a good doctor.'

'He'll tell me I'm pregnant.'

Abortion? Oh, it might be 1935, and doubtless there were 'moderns' up in Dublin prepared to wink the eye, but down here the very notion would have sent a tremor through the foundations of the mansions and mini-mansions of Upper Glenmorris.

'And also to do an advanced secretarial course,' he added. 'Then, if things are as you suppose, and I think you may be jumping to conclusions far too soon, we can get — it — adopted through a society.' He scarcely felt that it was his own flesh and blood that he was giving away. It was all too — irregular. He noted her fingers straying to her breast. Just as Vera's sometimes had done before the birth of Jim. Vera had complained of enlargement and tenderness.

'Mummy's always on to me about the glories of motherhood.' Her face was flushed with bitterness. 'Now it seems I'm to forego my success.' She had been vaguely aware over the past few days of a two-way thrust in her mind. One side of her head seemed to be against the other. What was it? What was it?

49

He stared at her, a startled expression in his brown eyes. 'If you pray to Jesus, he'll forgive you.'

'Jesus?' She murmured the word. Did Jesus really enter into her life, in the way that he did into Dodo's? Well, at least she believed that there was a God of some sort.

'If you want us to conceal things from Vera,' he said, 'and you may well be right — it would be a terrible thing for her to have to face — that means we must also conceal it from your mother. Otherwise, once the matter is out, it's out. Besides, it could hardly be less terrible for your mother.'

Mummy! Mummy had once annoyed her by roguishly hinting that Dodo's feelings were more than fatherly. Even so, should she ever find out about the baby, surely she would suspect that it was Jim's. Dodo awaited her reply. 'I'll go to Dublin.'

There wasn't much conviction. Nevertheless, somewhat relieved, he moved, still in his squatting position, more directly in front of her. His broad fist gripped her folded hands. 'We must get you away as quickly as we can.' He heard her chair move. Her eyes were large. 'I occasionally go up to Dublin on business, as you know. We'll go up together —' There was something peculiar in the way she was staring at him. 'We'll find a flat for you. I'll be able to stay at a nearby hotel until you feel settled in. I'll be able to get up to visit you from time to time. You'll find —' *Was* she staring at him? Or — *was she looking over his shoulder*? Suddenly he knew that it hadn't been her chair that had moved. It had been the door that had opened. He looked round and upwards. In the doorway, pale and still, looking down at him from his great height, stood his son.

Earlier that Saturday afternoon Jim had been out on his bicycle. He had leaned the machine against a snow-covered bank. He had pulled back the carrier's spring clip and released an old mackintosh, which he spread on the bank. Extracting a sketching pad and a case of charcoal pencils from one of the two paniers, he sat down. How the darkness of Jenny's eyes contrasted with the gold of her hair! How the alternating moods of defiance and diffidence chased one another across her face!

Before him, steps rose steeply to the black weather-slated house high above the road. A for-sale notice was pasted on a window downstairs. What a home it would make for someone! He felt again his incompleteness. Perhaps it was due to his dissatisfaction with his art. His charcoal pencil moved over the surface of the rough paper.

The cold began to nip his fingers and ears. He stared at his sketch. He found that he had doodled in a bridegroom carrying his bride across the threshold. Abruptly he rose. The light was almost gone; his watch showed half past four. Saturday being a whole holiday at the printers', Jenny would be at home. He mounted. His tyres sank with a muffled crunch into a puffy carpet. He felt the need to speak to her. A lace curtain of falling snow was suddenly drawn about him. The white earth rose at the brim of the horizon to meet the burdened sky.

Mrs Byrne, a cigarette gripped in the side of her mouth, was playing Patience at the table in the dining-room cum drawing-room when she heard the call of, 'Anyone at home?' So Jim was looking for Jenny! How delightful! Recently she had feared that he was hanging back.

She threw a coquettish glance at the handsome young man, his long legs elegant in narrow whipcord trousers, who had sauntered into the room. She put down the cards. 'Jenny took some office papers over to Karachi House, Jim. If you're cycling, you'll catch her up.' Her wrists jingled as she stooped and picked up one of her little dogs. 'And did he do his business on the grass patch?' She kissed the small head. 'Does he always look for a grass patch on which to do his little business?'

Jim laughed and left. He rather liked Mrs Byrne, flattered by her worship of males and her vast regard for his social position.

He cycled along cautiously, his face livid in the snow-light. A figure ahead was turning in through the gate of Karachi House. It was still only a little over two months since he had returned to Glenmorris and got to know her all over again. 'Jenny!' She didn't hear. he pressed hard on the pedal. There was a slithering of the back wheel, a wobble of the front, his leading tyre buried itself in a snow drift at the roadside — and he was off.

It was a cushioned fall. But, by the time he reached the drawing-room door, the murmur of voices told him that it was too late to speak while his resolution was still warm. Should he interrupt them? Strange that his father hadn't taken her into his study where he

51

usually transacted business! A drawing-room was, after all, a public room. He pushed open the door.

The phrases: 'we must get you away as quickly as we can', 'we'll go up together', 'I'll be able to get up to visit you from time to time', turned round and round in his head. Why should she go to Dublin? An extension of her business training? But why such urgent language? Why such assurances of his father's company? He stared at the latter's peculiar attitude, at the great fist covering Jenny's hands. It couldn't be . . . No, of course not. Their demeanour towards one another had changed completely. Then why those two frozen faces turned towards him? He saw that Jenny had drawn away her hands.

'Oh, hello Jim!' It was painful to watch the usually confident face turned upon him uncertainly, the deep-set eyes trying to read how much he had heard, the moustache twitching to recover its authority and to give the impression that its owner had been engaged on business of a reputable, if private, nature. His father remained squatting a moment to avoid the effect of a guilty scramble to his feet. 'Were you looking for me?'

'No, I wasn't.' He turned to leave. He struck his shoulder against the edge of the door and, in recoiling, collided with the door-post. He hardly noticed the double jar. He closed the door. So much for his hope that he might resurrect her once-offered companionship! Here she was, turning to his father in some matter of apparent stress.

Henry stood motionless. What had he been saying as the boy had come in? Words that would have told him that his father was sending Jenny to Dublin. Nothing there for more than surprise at the most. He remembered his hand on Jenny's. Surely the boy didn't think . . . Impossible, on the strength of so insignificant an act. Unless he had noticed anything before. Had he, down the years, been reading his father better than his father had been able to read himself?

'Jenny, why didn't you warn me?'

She was still staring at the door. 'He heard.'

'He ken't have heard anything about the . . .' His face grey, he gazed at her.

She stood up. 'I'm done for.'

'Ah, for goodness sake . . .' They were *all* done for if she didn't pull herself together. 'I realise you've passed nearly all your life in

52

Glenmorris. But ken't you ketch on to the opportunities outside?'

'Mummy would expect me back for Christmas. She'd sell something if necessary to get me back. Or she'd visit me.'

In the hall, Jim drew out the cheroot case that his mother had given him. In the spirals of the smoke, clues eddied out of the past. He had once said jokingly to Jenny, 'I wonder who's taken my place in your life? Can't guess, although you're so exclusive. You never seem to move outside the circle in which you grew up.'

'Didn't you notice, what with being abroad so much, how few here are our sort of people?'

Few indeed! Dangerously few . . .

'Hello, darling!' It was his mother. There she stood, to him an angel in an evening gown. Her thick brown hair, the few strands of grey giving her dignity, framed those gentle features he loved so well. A subtle scent stole to his nostrils. In her hands, protected by gardening gloves, were a pot of geraniums and a torch. 'Are you feeling all right?' Knowing his dislike of being fussed over she added quickly, 'Would you close the front door behind me. I always think that one of the delights of a greenhouse is the way you have flowers in the middle of winter.'

He gazed at her, his heart in eyes as blue as hers. They were never more than half a thought apart. Tears pricked his eyes. A lovely lady! He understood the desolation for her of his empty nursery on the day he had gone to his first boarding-school; the pain she had had to bear when his adolescent masculine aggressiveness had caused him to treat her with surliness; or when, as a young man, he had fled her home. He had sensed that she liked to be seen in public walking, elegant, at his side. He would walk at her side all the rest of her days.

'I was on my way,' she said, 'to put this pot in the drawing-room.' She had advanced half a dozen steps.

'Mother, let me take it in for you.'

Voices came from behind the door. 'Isn't that Jenny?' She drew back the pot. 'I'm so glad she's here. It'll help buck Dad up. They're always so gay when they are together.' She pushed open the door. Jim watched her features, caught in the glitter of the chandelier. 'Hello, Jenny!' Vera studied the young girl a moment. Was there a pinkness about the eyes? 'Is anything the matter?'

'No, Mrs Hampton. It was just some office papers I brought over. I . . .'

Henry's moustache moved. Jenny was looking at his wife with more than anxiety; with remorse too. Would the girl break down?

Vera's blue eyes still studied them. Both seemed rather pale. Come to think of it, she had missed of late his demands to know: Vera, why ken't you be like Jenny?

Henry watched her closely. With her sense of character, did she see that something was wrong? Or did her need to believe in her family cloud her vision? There was a footstep. He looked round. Jim again stood in the doorway, his jaw set. Had the boy told her anything?

'Jenny, come and see the sketch I did this afternoon.'

Henry saw his son smile, but draw on his cheroot, as always when nervous.

The sound of Jenny's closing the drawing-room door behind her was the signal for Jim to wheel round. He blew out a ring of smoke at the peacock feathers and tribal spears decorating the hall. 'You're not to go on seeing my father. I don't know what you're up to, but you're up to something.'

Her eyes were large under their golden fringe. 'Jim, there was nothing happening, in the way that you mean.' She raised the office papers. 'Your father was persuading me to take a secretarial course in Dublin.'

'On his knees! Baloney! Why should you need a secretarial course? You've had a secretarial course.'

'*You've* had courses in printing and art, but is there nothing more for you to learn?' The touch of spirit seemed to exhaust what remained of her courage. She sank on to a chair, her face in her hands. The papers spilled on to the floor.

His jolt at the way she had rounded on him altered to alarm. Was she going to faint? His mother might at any moment walk out of that door five paces away. 'My sketch is outside in my cycle panier.'

As he picked up the papers, she leaned forward to help him. He looked at her. What a charming face! He had never really noticed before just how charming. And all the more appealing for its distress.

She tried to rise.

'Here, lean on me. You'll feel better in the night air.'

The bite of the cold steadied his own head also. By the light of the open door he undid the panier. 'I always keep my sketches, especially my nudes, well strapped up. I don't want them to be seen by all and, particularly, sundry. I can't bear Sundry to see my nudes; he's such a tittle-tattle.' His fingers slowed, then ceased to move. He rested his hands on the bicycle saddle. 'What's happening, Jenny?'

She was putting on her gloves, the office papers tucked under her arm. 'In the way that you think, nothing, nothing, nothing.'

Well, that squared with their immediate past behaviour. He looked at her steadily. 'I came to ask you to be friends. I'm afraid I snubbed you in the past. I was very stupid.'

'Oh no, Jim. I was only a schoolgirl.'

'You're very beautiful.'

She stared at him. 'Jim, d'you really —'

'You're very beautiful.'

'I wish you'd said that sooner.' She buried her face in her gloves. Her shoulders trembled.

He heard his parents' voices. In a few strides he was back at the door. He closed it quietly. Returning, he clasped her shoulders. 'What is it, Jenny?' This urgent planning to send her to Dublin! Was she ill? Then why wasn't her mother with her? Was it something that she had to conceal from Mrs Byrne?

The brass Indian gong boomed in the hall.

'I must go in at once,' he said. 'They mustn't come out here looking for me. Now you go straight home before my mother can ask you to dinner. Don't you worry about a single thing. We'll straighten it all out tomorrow after church.' Voices sounded in the hall. He gave her a little push. 'Quick! Quick!'

She hurried away over the snow, the fur collar of her coat clutched about her ears and chin. Once out of sight of Karachi House, she paused. She gazed at the dim shape of King William Fort, sleeping aggessively like a grey dragon, battlemented, turretted, cannoned, ready it seemed to wake with a roar in defence of the harbour. With Jim she had once upon a time crossed the grassy dike guarding the fort on its landward side. The gaps in the rotting planks of the bridge had afforded a glimpse of the supporting girders, here and there fallen away into a ruin of rust. They had passed through the stone gateway, with slits in its massive walls as firing points. They had strolled through the tangle of overgrown courtyards. They had poked their heads into the windowless and roofless buildings, gutted with fire by nationalists the moment the British garrison had moved out. Together they had mounted on to a paved sentry-beat and paced round its semi-circle. The bank on their left-hand side was high enough to protect the sentry, yet not so high as to obscure his view of the approaches to the harbour. In a single lithe movement Jim had dug his toe into the bank and mounted it. He had stretched down his hand to assist her up. Side by side they had stood on the grass-covered summit of the bastion, over their heads a calm summer sky and, far below, the sea lapping over harsh weed-covered rocks. Those savage rocks . . .

She resumed walking.

As Jim sat down at the dining-room table, gazed at by surrounding portraits of ancestors, he said, 'She decided she must go home.'

'Oh,' put in Vera, 'she would have been very welcome to join us.'

Henry glanced at his son. What had the boy been saying to Jenny?

Later Vera went to the kitchen. 'Bring me the coffee-pot, Bridie. I'll make the coffee myself.' She eyed the servant with distrust where she stood humped over the sink. Her feet, in their split-apart shoes, cowed under the vast aggregation of flesh that they were called upon to support, clung spiritlessly to the stone-flagged floor — roots. Nevertheless the girl was flighty. She must be flighty. They were all flighty, here today and gone tomorrow. Bridie had been with her fourteen years.

Back in the dining-room Henry said, 'Jim, Jenny came to see me this evening in a rather hysterical state. Some difficulty at home.' The half truth was disagreeable. No more baloney. No more moral lisping. But what could he do? 'I'm thinking of sending her up to Dublin on a course.'

'I understand, Dad.'

Henry's heart lightened. The boy had been quite cordial!

Jim cycled cautiously down the hill, his headlight a crystalline bar sweeping the snow, the air biting at his ears. On the quay, two fishermen emerged from the pub. One carried a small sack out of which bulged tinned stores. Their unshaven faces, brick-brown from sea breezes and sunnier shores, looked devilish. They shambled past with slouched shoulders, their caps pulled down to their eyebrows, their blue sweaters torn, the one wearing much patched corduroys, the other much patched blue canvas trousers. Wild as the sea on which they toiled they seemed. Perhaps they found peace in its tumult.

He propped his bicycle by the pub door. The landlord, a man with smiling whiskers, served his sherry. So it was some difficulty at home with which Jenny had to contend! What could that be? Mrs Byrne was jolly, and devoted to her daughter — or at least to her interests.

The two ferry men had their faces in glasses of Guinness. The ferry crossed the river, shimmering in season with bass and salmon, that emptied into the inner harbour. On Sundays in particular they laboured at their long clumsy oars, the part of the shafts between the thole-pins, and the narrow blades, bound with steel tape. The boat was weighted down almost to the gunwales with its standing passengers on their way to Mass. Some of the men even had to perch on the gunwales, the seats of their blue serge trousers splashed by the wavelets. But all were fisher folk, and there was never an accident.

Was it money trouble? But if it were that, then surely it would have been Mrs Byrne herself who would have gone to see his father. No, Jenny was being sent up to Dublin to get her away from home. And urgently. Because she was ill? What need to conceal illness from her mother. Because she had committed some crime, stolen something? What need had she to steal. In any case his father would have made good the loss.

He finished his drink and emerged. Stars trembled like sequins on a black velvet gown. He wheeled his bicycle through a fine pillared doorway with a cracked fanlight, and into the passage. Leaning it against the wall, he passed a chain round one of the front forks and the rim of the wheel and padlocked it. He climbed the staircase to his attic studio. There he pressed down the switch. The blue-tinted bulb flooded the studio with its mock daylight, designed not to distort the colours of his pigments.

So — no money trouble, no illness, no crime. What remained? Was — was she going to have a — a baby? Of course not. Rubbish. Nonsense. There was his imagination, as usual rushing to extremes!

He picked up his brush. He would speak reassuringly to her in the morning. What would his mother make of all this, his mother of the blue perceptive eyes clouded by love?

At Karachi House, Henry stopped pencilling lines on his blotter. He rose from his work table in the corner of the drawing-room. 'Just going over to see Jenny.' He picked up the ledger. It would maintain appearances not only with Vera, but also with Mildred.

'What, again!'

'Silly of me! I forget something.'

Her needles resumed clicking. She tried to read the book on her knee. In the jumping firelight, the worry lines had deepened. 'Wrap up well.'

The snow scattered under his rapid stride; the Byrnes went to bed early. Mildred would indeed, as Jenny had pointed out, be able to afford to visit her in Dublin. But suppose he sent her to London? He had the precedent of sending Jim there. He must let the girl know at once; she might do something foolish in the night . . .

Their house was in darkness. His uneasiness sharpened, he walked home. Just before he turned in at his gate, he paused. He stared down at the thin string of lights on the quay. They glinted on the inky waters that stretched away into outer mystery. From boyhood days, when he had gone out fishing with his father, the sea and its depths had had power to pierce through the wall of his un-imaginativeness. How clean was its surface, how foul out there in the harbour it was below! How it could swallow up all foulness and bury it in its depths! Except when a receding spring tide drained parts of the harbour, exposing black sewage-fouled mud, tins, broken crockery, and fish carcases tossed in off the quay by the fishermen — carcases upon which crabs crawled in their silent feast . . .

He had prayed, if it were God's will, that his deed should not bring unhappiness to those he had wronged. God had not heard him. Or perhaps it was just that God did not act in that way. His laws were as they were, because to disregard them brought inevitable evil. The darkness caught Henry by the throat and stared with black eyes into his soul.

Chapter Five

Jenny sat on the edge of her bed. Yes, that's what she would like; a plate filled to the edge with porridge, brown sugar and cream. When she had asked for it one day, her mother had looked surprised. 'A girl has to watch her figure if she wants to catch a husband,' she had laughed. She had got her the porridge. But when Jenny had asked for it again a day later, her mother's glance, she thought, had been a little sharp. The foetus was a parasite, imposing on her these fancies just to feed itself. No, no, it was a part of her body. She could see the glinting brown granules of sugar, the rich cream. She dared not ask again.

Nausea seized her. She rose abruptly and bent over the beflowered china basin on the wash-hand stand. Usually she was sick only in the mornings, but a bad smell was enough at any time. Some milk had gone sour. She emptied it into the basin and washed out the cup. She listened to the tap of her mother's heels below. It had not paused. She poured water into the basin and disposed of its contents at the toilet along the passage.

Yesterday's Sunday church service had come and gone. Dodo had seemed to be hovering. She didn't want to be cornered by him, perhaps because the ugly relationship between them became emphasised by close proximity. Or perhaps because, in so far as she could not feel confidence in his Dublin plan, she regarded him as a broken staff. She kept close to Jim, only to discover that he was hovering too. *He* could not help either, for he couldn't be told.

It was a relief when the padre had approached, rubbing his hands. 'Lovely mixture of sunshine and sharp air!' He scrutinised her. 'Look down in the dumps, young lady! What about Jim and you coming for a drive? Parson on holiday kindly taken over my evening service for me. Give the parishioners a rest from my ugly face!'

In the same half minute she had noted Henry's concern, heard Jim's quick acceptance, and failed to resist the insistence of the genial autocrat. How had she ever got through that longest of all afternoons, filled with the padre's banter and Jim's probing? Had Jim discovered?

Her thoughts returned to the present. Women could lose their lives in childbirth . . . That was all far off and academic. She put on her coat; there was something much less far off and academic to be done.

She paused at the sitting-room door. 'I'm going for a short walk.'

Her mother continued to flick a card, grown grubby in her interminable games of Patience, first here then there; she was used to Jenny's solitary rambles. 'Put on your gloves, dear.' The long ash, shaken as she spoke, fell from the cigarette gripped between her lips and scattered itself over the cards.

Jenny's eyes lingered on her mother. She crossed the room and kissed her cheek.

Mildred looked up and smiled her pleasure. Jenny wasn't often so demonstrative. 'Perhaps you might call in and see Jim.'

'Perhaps.' Good old Mummy, matrimonially scheming to the end! To the end . . .

She hurried down the zig-zag road. At its harbour foot, she paused under a street lamp that shone on the fountain in the farm courtyard. In summer days the fountain showered down jewels on rainbow fish. Now the boy statue, as he poured water out of a gourd into a black pool, wore a cap of snow. Six yew trees, a white tinsel on them, stood around the pond like Christmas trees. The road divided. She glanced to her right, towards Lower Glenmorris and Jim in his attic perch. She turned about and gazed towards the shadowy bulk of King William Fort, with its rearing bastion and the sheer drop to the green-brown rocks. She made her way rapidly towards it. Perhaps she didn't feel in the mood for conversation.

Back at home, Mildred had ceased to place the cards on the table. She stared into the jumping fire. Somehow she felt that Jenny wasn't quite being herself. There had been that other time . . .

Henry finished sipping his coffee from the rose-decorated delicate china cup. He replaced it beside Vera's on the hammered-brass Afghan tray. The ledger under his arm, he hurried to Jenny's home.

At church, his sadness towards Jim had been replaced by irritation at his son's frustrating his need to talk to Jenny. It was essential to prevent her doing anything desperate during the night. The young people nowadays had no balance, no — regularity.

When Mildred Byrne, with a naive glance of admiration and a tossing of scent from her hair in his direction (doubtless he was admiring her milkmaid compexion) informed him that Jenny had gone out ten minutes previously, certainly down to the quay and probably to Jim's studio, he broke into a sweat. Would he never be able to ketch hold of the dratted girl! For appearances' sake he remained five minutes longer, sitting on the edge of his chair and enduring the yapping. The two dogs had retreated under the hem of Mildred's skirt, from which unassailable bastion they continued their harassment. Forgetting his principle of mercy towards God's lesser creatures, he found relief by mentally bashing their heads together. *They* were not *dogs!* Overbred smelly little creatures, with their high-drawn bodies and protruding eyes!

Passing out through the narrow hall, he glanced at Jenny's water-colour of the racing yachts rounding the red bulk of Masterman buoy. Descending the hill, he strode on to the quay past the shelter formed with a sheet of corrugated iron supported by rough un-painted wooden posts, and lighted by a lantern. Superannuated fishermen, seated on the bench within, sucked at clay pipes. They tipped their caps. Were they staring curiously at him? He hastened on. No light came from the studio windows, but the street lamp revealed that the shutters were closed. He would have to wait for the girl to come out, otherwise Jim might ketch on. If she were behind those shutters, all would be well. If not, he wouldn't know where to look. Was it proper for her to be there at all?

A quarter of an hour earlier Jim had thrown down his brush. He stared at the closed shutters. He must walk; feel the bite of the snow. He pulled on his coat and black sombrero, switched out the blue-tinted bulb, and descended. He turned along the quay in the direction of Upper Glenmorris. Ahead, a road light picked out the fountain and the snow-capped boy statue. A woman's figure appeared in the light for an instant, then turned away along the harbour road. Surely he knew that lissom form? He opened his mouth, then closed it again. She was now a distant figure in the light of the moon. She must have been walking at a tremendous pace; even his great stride hardly closed the gap. It *couldn't* be she! Why should she be out at that late hour? He halted.

His previous decision, to see Jenny at her home, had weakened. She'd only fend him off again. What would he be able to do, with her mother there? He returned along the quay.

The light by the slip shone on a handsome broken fanlight and the tall figure of a man. The man, wearing his seafaring cap doubtless for warmth, strode up and down jerkily, beating his gloved hands together. His shadow on the roadway now swelled up into a giant, now shrank into a dark pool at his feet. Jim approached him, moving his palm in the sweeping gesture of greeting. His father's stare spoke of an uncharacteristic panic.

'Oh Jim, didn't Jenny — er — was Jenny here?' He brandished the account book.

'Jenny?'

'Might she be waiting for you on the stairs?'

His son stabbed a finger at him. 'The girl on the harbour road!'

Possessed of the facts, Henry began to stride along the quay.

Jim followed and caught his sleeve. 'What is it, Dad?'

Urgency and caution, struggling together in Henry's broad breast, finally produced the words in a subdued burst. 'She's going to do herself some mischief.'

Jim stared. Suicide? Jenny of the athletic body and the sea wind in her hair! Baloney! Crime? Disease? She had not looked ill; rather of late she seemed to have acquired a greater buxomness. Buxomness . . . A baby? But with what man had she ever associated in that way?

'You'll never catch her like this, Dad. I've my bike.'

Henry halted. 'Wish I'd driven down in the car, but the snow . . .'

Jim sprinted back towards the studio. What man? What man?

Henry watched his son, as he rode past him a few minutes later, give the pedals a backward turn to free the cogs of the gearbox as he changed from low into middle gear. The brim of the sombrero threw a shadow over the lean features bent over the handlebars.

'Stop her by force if necessary.' Would the boy ketch his meaning?

He saw him nod in understanding before he became a diminishing figure in the moonlight. How he had acted without pressing for reasons! Sudden horror seized Henry. What right would he have to be warmed by the sun and to hear the cry of the gulls, if a young girl lay cold in the ground with stopped ears?

A splash of light on a fountain caused Jim to look up. His eyes had been set on the revolutions of his front wheel, as he guarded against a skid in the snow. His ears had been filled with the crunching of his tyres. The glistening white surface was broken now only by the marks of passage of two bicycles, a pedestrian, and a dog.

So it was because of this baby that she had gone to his father! His father would have the money and the influence to send her away to Dublin. That could mean only that she was hiding her pregnancy from her mother. Otherwise it would have been Mrs Byrne, more likely, who would have gone to see his father.

A road turned off inland from the harbour road, drawing away with it the tracks of the bicycles. Only those of the pedestrian and the dog remained. Presently even the paw marks disappeared in a scattering of snow, where the dog had rushed up the bank in pursuit of adventure. The single track of footprints kept determinedly on. He pressed down harder on the pedals.

How long had he been back from Paris and London? Two months only. This calamity might well have derived from some earlier time when he couldn't have known with whom she was associating. Abortion? He shuddered. Abortion in this year of 1935 was vaguely associated in his mind with sleazy city back-street practitioners and working girls dying of sepsis or haemorrhage. What had a church-going country gentry got to do with abortion (though doubtless there were exceptions)? Contretemps of this sort were usually solved by marriage or leaving the neighbourhood.

The moon, in the unutterable purity of its perfect circle and cold whiteness, hung in silence in the sky, icily aloof. Its radiance spilled upon the snow, picking out sharply the single track of footprints that travelled on and on across a dead and muffled world. The feet of the traveller had sunk deep, each step an effort, but purposeful steps. Ahead, King William Fort came into view, its bastion rearing up from the stillness of the sea. Before the terror of its stark menace, Jim suddenly knew with a total certainty that he wanted Jenny. O

God (in his anguish, he reverted by habit to the cry of his childhood) that she might be alive!

What man? Someone outside Glenmorris? Not likely. She was so exclusive. His — his father? Of course not. Quite unthinkable. He was too religious a man. Jenny was too fond of his mother.

He leapt joyfully off his bicycle. 'Jenny!'

The tall figure that had just rounded the corner ahead paused.

'It — it's a beautiful night, isn't it?' she ventured.

He discerned surprise and caution. Suicide? Codswallop! His father had been exaggerating things. She had obviously been out on one of her perfectly usual solitary rambles, if much later than usual.

She spoke again. 'Were you — were you out getting ideas for a picture?'

He saw her eyes still probing him. They were steady, resolute, but shadowed with fatigue.

His illusion of normality began to falter. 'You've got some snow on your coat.' How to introduce to her his knowledge, and his wish to help?

'Oh! I sat down for a while.' She banged at herself.

'I told Dad I'd seen you out walking. He was worried about you.'

Her scrutiny sharpened. 'Why?'

His anxiety sharpened too. But he must press on. 'He said he was afraid you were going to do yourself a mischief.'

In the confusing light of the moon, he imagined that the colour had flared into her cheeks. 'Why should he think that?'

Was her anger, apart from her usual high spirit, due to a desperate need to conceal . . . 'You're going to have a baby, aren't you?'

She was standing very still.

He lifted round his bicycle. 'Let's go home.'

They walked in silence. Thus Henry found them as he appeared, running, in the beam of the bicycle lamp. He pulled off his cap. The droplets of moisture glistened on his brow.

He smiled in the very force of his relief. 'Well, Jenny, you gave us — er — you're out walking late in this cold weather!'

'I just wanted to get away by myself for a little.' Dodo's company was now welcome; he was someone who didn't judge her.

Henry elected to walk, not beside her, but beside his son, the bicycle between them. He rested his hand for an instant on the saddle.

It touched Jim's. He felt the latter wince away. The boy knew! He had lost his son. How much did he know?

At the fountain he paused. 'You'll be wanting to get back to your studio, Jim. I'll see Jenny home.'

He watched his son pondering.

'All right.' Jim turned the front wheel in the direction of the quay. He pushed off and mounted. If not his father, then what other man? The absence of any other likely candidate stared back at him with unwinking eyes.

He jumped off. Catching hold of the saddle and handlebars, he fairly whirled the machine round through the air. Pushing it violently over the snow, he strode up to Jenny.

'So this is your idea of repaying my mother for her years of kindness!' His voice was thick in his chest. All his feeling for her seemed dead.

She drew back, her eyes large. 'What — what d'you mean?'

'You know what I mean.' Henry caught the quick glance at himself.

She put out her gloved hand behind her and felt for the bank. She sank down on the snow. Elbows resting on her lap, hands folded together, head bowed, she seemed to Henry to await whatever storm was about to break upon her.

He watched his son poised quivering, like an eagle undecided whether or not to swoop. Perhaps the demonstration that she suffered remorse would tie his wings.

Suddenly she spoke. 'Don't you understand how natural a thing, how little a moment, can bring it all about?'

'Oh, that's all my eye and Betty Martin!' How soft her cheeks, how soft and full her body! Full of . . .

Henry took a step forward. Doubtless the boy was seeing the gentle face of his mother and a dozen instances of her consideration for Jenny.

His son's eyes still blazed. 'My mother always dispensed loyalty and affection and simplicity. And her reward? Cynicism, intrigue!'

'Jim, the responsibility was mine, hardly Jenny's at all. I was by so much the elder.'

He saw the blue eyes turn on him. 'Yes, indeed it was! So much for your religion! Not even your lack of self-awareness could conceal from you so crude a contradiction.'

To be judged by the son he had once, so short a time ago it seemed, held in his arms, a little trusting bundle smelling of warm wool and baby powder! He could not tell him of his loneliness for Vera. Honour thy father and thy mother . . . What chance had he given the boy? 'There's nothing wrong with my religion, Jim. It was I that didn't measure up to it.'

The blue eyes considered him, then returned to Jenny. Appalled before the gaunt disaster that reared over his home, Jim forced out the words. 'We must say the baby's mine. We must marry.'

The idea spread over his mind like the black sewage-fouled mud that the withdrawing tide exposed. A son marrying his father's mistress, and purporting to be the father of his own half-brother! Almost a suggestion of incest! The stock-yard brought into the intimate delicacies of a home! His mother, lover of her family, of old leather-bound books and the fragile sheen of afternoon teacups, of lavender-filled bags to scent the blouses in the drawers of her dressing-table, forced to play a role in this farmyard drama!

He tried to whittle down the unpleasantness of it. After all, it *wasn't* incest. As far as his father's relations with Jenny were concerned, they amounted to no more than an infidelity such as occurred in thousands every year. If he himself took such measures as were necessary to save his mother's feelings and his father's reputation, that must be counted an act of filial piety.

He repeated more determinedly, 'We must marry.'

She shook her head. 'I'm going to Dublin to have it there. I'll get it adopted.' She spoke at random. Had she no faith in the scheme?

Henry watched her. Had she seen the relief showing in the boy's face? How humiliating for her! Yet how could the boy want to be fathered with a child so conceived? How could he wish to be embarrassed with his mother, claiming the paternity?

Jim turned his bicycle. 'Tomorrow I'll find out what you've decided. I'll support your plans where necessary.' As he rode away he flung back over his shoulder, 'But I won't let my position slip into that of a co-conspirator.' Ahead of him drifts of moonlight gilded the sea and turned the still fields to milk.

*   *   *

66

Henry stood staring after his departing son. The boy would never tell his mother; there were some secrets so terrible that they buried themselves. Jenny therefore still remained the crux. Wearied though he was, he must drive on to a solution. He dipped deep, and found some store left of that magnificent energy which had never yet failed him. He proposed his London plan.

'But Mummy,' she said, 'might still manage to raise the fare.'

'She won't expect you this Christmas when you've only just gone. We must meet each difficulty as it comes.'

'I wish I were going now. Sooner or later I'll be sick at the table.'

Henry's lips were compressed. 'I'd better see your mother straight away.' He added suddenly, 'Jenny — this evening — you weren't contemplating . . .'

She considered. 'For myself, yes. But I've someone else now in my care.'

Henry glanced at her, startled even more by the second statement than the first. 'It would have been a sin.' He spoke more to himself than to her.

Jenny's eyes were far away. That two-way thrust in her mind! That one side of her head against the other! Because of the affection which Vera had borne her, she had been filled with horror at her pregnancy. Filled — but not quite. Deep in the tangle of her mind, in some half glimpsed primal glade older than all the moralities, lurked a secret bodily delight that she had fulfilled the purpose for which she had been structured.

When Mildred sought a postponement of her daughter's departure because of shopping to be done, Henry irritably popped a boiled sweet into his mouth. Couldn't the dratted woman get it into her head that Glenmorris and Cork were not the world's only two shopping centres? Well, she *was* after all a mother, and behold what he had done to her child! What right had he to criticise her? Was she looking after his property, though . . .

He gave his usual covert glance of disgust at the chair before sitting down. It was covered with the hairs of those artificial over-bred creatures, one of which was yapping at him from under the table, its bony high-drawn body trembling, its eyes strained and protruding. He stretched out his hand to pacify it. It retreated wildly under Mildred's skirts. Panic raised its voice to a shriller pitch.

'Be quiet, Gordon, you silly boy!' She picked it up. 'And does he want to do his little business on the grass patch?'

A new anxiety gripped her. Did this sending of Jenny to London portend an effort to break up any possible growing intimacy with Jim? No, no. Henry had spoken categorically of its being a training trip. But there was the frightful possibility that Jim might take up with some other girl. Yet if Henry were crossed, he might dismiss Jenny. That would mean her getting a job in Cork. How much less would she see Jim then! Henry, from being a patron, might become an enemy.

'Could,' he said, 'she be ready in three days? I'm crossing over on business myself. I want to persuade the London wholesalers to handle our publications. *The Hotel & Boarding-house Register* should appeal to the tourist industry.' He made a considerable effort to convince himself that it would be a good stroke of business; fragments of the old Henry survived in the new.

'All right. But I hope that Jenny will be protected from bad company. Of course she'll be in trustworthy hands while *you* are there.'

Henry's moustache moved.

On his return to Karachi House, he found his wife at the fireside. 'But,' cried Vera, 'we're putting up that representative of the Church Mission to Bechuanaland! I can't entertain him alone. It would look most rude.'

He pressed his lips together, then rapidly assumed a smile. 'Tch! I'd forgotten all about him.'

'What — what is this business in London?'

'Oh, it can wait.' He couldn't have pretended otherwise. 'Just exploring the possibility of getting our publications sold by the London newsagents and bookstalls.' It would mean a delay of a further week; ten days in all. He shifted in his armchair; her blue eyes were scrutinising him, as earlier had Jim's. Was she noting, as his mirror had, that his face was thinner, the angles of brow and jaw more pronounced?

'Oh yes of course,' she said. 'That can be done at any time.' Considerately, she moved her eyes away. His stride seemed less brisk, as though he had lost his sense of direction. He was behaving almost — almost as though he felt guilty . . . 'It's strange, old fellow, that you never mentioned this plan of sending Jenny to London.' She smiled to soften the reproof. 'Henry — Henry, is everything all right with her? When I came into the drawing-room that time . . . Jim was there . . . I felt — I don't know . . .'

Henry's lips were bloodless. 'Don't you remember, about six months ago we were discussing the possibility of sending her away for further training?' The words tumbled over one another.

Moral lisping? Baloney? But what else could he do? Could Jenny go unescorted? Mildred would object. Also it would look so odd, if he himself were travelling over in ten days. It was essential to avoid the appearance of urgency.

'But that,' said Vera, 'was only a vague idea, and to Cork or Dublin.'

'Ah, for goodness sake, woman!' His attempt at a remonstration was unconvincing. Could he get over to London with Jenny before the guest arrived, settle her in, and be back in time? Impossible. 'I've only just mentioned the scheme to Jenny herself.' He added, on a sudden inspiration, 'Jim did very well in London.'

'I think that Jim and Jenny may miss one another.'

'It's only for a year.'

'A year's a long time at that age.'

Henry's face brightened. 'Why shouldn't Jim take Jenny over?'

Her worried frown left her. 'And it will help to keep them together in spirit. By the way, Henry, you'll have to perform your usual execution.' She made a face of mock revulsion. 'The cat has had her kittens. She's ignored the box I've made ready for her and taken them out into the garden.'

He extracted an electric torch from the drawer of the hall-stand. Outside, feeble voices caught his ear. They came from a flower-bed beside the tennis court. Even when he was right up to the bed he could see nothing of them. Even when he was right upon the plant from which the voices issued, he still could see nothing. He lifted up the thick drooping leaves. The cat, her gold-flecked eyes burning back at him as they reflected the light of his torch, lay on her side. A mass of miniature cats struggled for her milk, turning their blind faces this way and that. He noted that the bald spot on the cat's forehead had become still larger. He would arrange for treatment. If she didn't improve, she might have to be put down by the vet.

He fetched from the pantry the picnic basket with the lid. Again lifting the leaves, he found the cat gone. The kittens were squeaking and climbing over one another. He saw two eyes burning in the darkness. The cat was watching him from ten paces away. His great practical hand transferred to the basket four thistle- down bodies; the animal could not be allowed to breed unchecked or the place would be overrun. The fifth kitten, which he had selected as the handsomest and strongest, he left. It would be cruelty to the animal wholly to remove its family. The cat shot past his hand into her nook. She settled down, purring, and received the remaining kitten to her, seemingly giving no thought to the rape of the others. She even stretched out her head as if inviting him to stroke it. Henry didn't do so. Cats were not for stroking; they were for keeping the property clear of mice. He closed the lid of the basket.

He started towards the kitchen. It was his intention to hold the kittens, one by one, under water in a basin. The vision of Bridie's red orb, gleefully watching, rose up before him distastefully. He got out the car. Switching on the headlights, he ran down the hill.

He stood, the basket in his hand, on the edge of the quay. The water, driven by a fresh breeze, ran by black and energetic nine feet below him. The uncertain beat of an engine arose. An old hulk, filled to the gunwhale with sand, slipped past. In the light of the few street lamps he made out the form of a shabby young fellow in a cloth cap crouched on top of his cargo, steering by a wooden tiller. The imbecile gave Henry his meaningless smile.

Henry made for the slip, opening the lid of the basket as he went. He looked at the tiny warm furry things. He was about to drown them! Drown . . . It would be soon over. Their heads held under by an irresistible force, so that their lungs filled in a moment . . . Very different from a man thrown out of a boat — swimming — swimming — surges of terror — exhausted muscles — head ever more often sinking beneath the pitiless waves — the bitter water finding its way in between the despairing lips . . .

Then Henry did a most extraordinary thing. He abruptly walked to the edge of the quay and tipped the feebly squealing kittens into the water. There were a number of light splashes, followed by absolute silence. One moment four little voices, the next, nothing, as though a hand had stretched out of the darkness and closed over

70

them. He couldn't discern the small black creatures in the shadowed waters.

He plucked his torch from his pocket and threw down a circle of light. It was with surprise that he saw how the limbs, that on shore had been too feeble to walk or even to stand, were able to strike out, albeit with no great strength, in the sea. The kittens' bodies floated like feathers on the very surface of the water, bobbing up and down with every ripple. They swam aimlessly hither and thither, and he reminded himself that they couldn't see. One was swimming straight for the wall formed by the side of the quay. Its claw clutched at some slight break in the surface and held on. How much longer would they continue to swim? Ah, for goodness sake . . . Was the animal about to support itself, by ketching on to the wall, perhaps for minutes on end? Surely the December coldness of the water could be counted on to quench the tiny spark of life!

What on earth had possessed him to do such a thing — he, one of the few fishermen in Glenmorris who took the pains to break the back of each mackerel as it was caught, to save it from a slow suffocation? To the consternation in his face was added pity. Poor little brutes, scarcely emerged from the safety of the womb, called upon so abruptly, without the guidance of an older animal, to make so unequal a bid to save themselves in a strange and giant world which they had not even seen!

Wind-driven, the current ran briskly by, carrying the kittens down the harbour. An eddy plucked the hold of the kitten from the wall and carried it away with the rest. The struggles quickly grew less. His last view of the creatures, as they passed out of the light of the torch, was of a kitten tilted forward with its head below the surface, and its tail, which had a white tip, stuck up into the air like a miniature mast.

He stared into the darkness after them. His tweed-jacketed chest rose and fell. Their struggles had been short. But they were but young creatures, their lives scarcely begun and easily snuffed out. Not strongly established as in a grown man . . . They hardly knew what was happening — not like a highly sentient being . . .

Chapter Six

'Take it away! Take it away!' The strangled cry emerged from the red-brick building with the board across its face reading, 'The Glenmorris Printing Company'.

The tall wide-shouldered figure striding along the quay halted. The blue eyes, under the brim of the black sombrero, turned sharply towards the sound of the girl's voice.

As Jim strode into the foyer, he found it filled with women in overalls. Through a door was a view of empty benches. The deserted tables were stacked with unbound book and magazine pages. A pot on an oil stove steamed gently. From the bristles of the brush laid across its top, a drop of warm glue dripped on to the table. In the centre of the melee towered Mrs O'Donovan, her grey corkscrews dancing agitatedly. She held high her basin of slops, like a priestess bearing a vessel of sacred oil.

'Mister Jim, Miss Jenny was starting up the stairs, meself standing aside with the slops in me hand, when Miss Jenny takes one look at them and runs over into the corner.'

He caught sight of a bowed head, golden locks falling over the cheeks. Jenny waved a hand, gloved with the fur gloves that Henry had given her, at the basin. 'Take it away! Take it away!'

Other voices took up the call. 'Take it away! 'Tis the basin that's upsetting her.'

Jim had hitherto scarcely troubled his head with the phenomena of pregnancy, but he knew sufficient. He pushed through the group, which respectfully parted for him.

Mrs O'Donovan evidently felt her responsibility. 'Doesn't she pass me every morning on them stairs, and never no harm done?' He heard her add, ''Tis something special that's wrong with her, surely.' Her eyes, grey as the coils of her hair, scrutinised Jenny.

'It's only something she's eaten.' He gave a sharp tug at the brim of his sombrero. 'Come on, Jenny! Here, take my handkerchief!'

Grasping it awkwardly in the thick glove, she held it to her mouth and nose. He piloted her up the scrubbed wooden stairs smelling of disinfectant. The rest had bustled Mrs O'Donovan aside. She still held her basin on high, repeating the incantation, ''Tis something special that's wrong with her.' But he had the satisfaction of hearing a consensus of voices saying, 'Aye, 'tis only something she ate for her breakfast, most likely.'

She sank on to her office chair. 'I was nearly sick. I'll have to tell Mummy. No one else.' There was a desperate tremble in her voice. 'I can't hold out.'

He whipped off his sombrero and threw it down on her desk. 'Get hold of yourself! Someone's coming. It's the least you owe my mother.'

The harsh appeal, the pain of his grip on her shoulder, steadied her. Hurriedly she passed him his handkerchief. She put her gloves down beside his hat.

He drew out the silver case. 'Will this upset you?' His fingers, the first two slightly stained, extracted a cheroot. He listened to the brisk stride ascending the stairs.

She looked up. 'No. I like them.'

He blew out scented smoke. The office, stark once more without the red roses, became invested with opulence and Continental romance.

Henry appeared. He had scarely slept. It had been a shameful thing, the way he had drowned those kittens. Shameful. He crossed his son's office and entered Jenny's. He examined Jim's wilful expression, the defiance of the unrestrained splendours of his waistcoat. As usual, he took the bull by the horns. 'Hello, Jenny!' The child was tense, of course, but otherwise seemed to have recovered. 'We'll have to tell Vera and your mother about your — upset. We ken't have them finding out from the gossip. I was going to ask Jim to take you to London. I'm tied up. We've a missionary coming to stay.'

'They musn't be told.' His son's voice was sharp. 'They may not hear about it. Why make sure that they do?'

'I mean to say . . . Your mother isn't living on the moon.'

His son was already picking up his hat and moving towards his office, his cheekbones reddening like his mother's. 'Jenny'll be leaving at once. I'll take her.'

He lingered a moment in the doorway until he heard their murmurs of assent.

Standing by his window. his long legs elegant in narrow trousers, he drew deep on his cheroot. The frozen slender poles of spruce on a hill across the harbour, standing in snow and seen through a haze, were a Grecian frieze in powder blue. The rising sun was reflected, a burning spark, in a window pane of one of the houses. There was the promise of a quick thaw. Jenny's deed was bringing its own retribution, without his adding to her burden. Had *he* never been improvident, and escaped more by good luck than by good management?

He crossed to his desk with the glass top that could be illuminated from below. He picked up a cut-out of a drawing he had made. With one finger he held it in place on the cover design for the next issue of *The Hotel & Boarding-house Register*, while with the other he took up his paste pot. It was empty. He remembered the pot of simmering glue in the binding department. Design in hand, he descended.

'Says she, "When I heard that Miss Jenny had felt sick, I couldn't but help it come into me mind."'

Jim paused on the step. The voice had reached him over the partitioning that formed the receptionist's office, protecting Eileen O'Herlihy from the draughts of the foyer.

Eileen O'Herlihy was continuing. Jim could imagine her luxuriant red hair tumbling on to her thin shoulders, her large brown eyes with red flecks in them. '"I've got six children of me own," says Mrs Sullivan, "four of them, God be praised, alive and well. I had a bad time with all of them. I'd heave if I saw a maggot in an apple." '

'Look at that, now!' It was the voice of Mrs O'Donovan,

'Them's her own words, "A maggot in an apple." '

'But in the case of such a nice respectable girl as Miss Jenny, one of the gentry —' Jim, with his mind's eye, saw the tight little steel-grey curls of Mrs O'Donovan nodding agitatedly.

'Oh, the gentry, the gentry!' The red-flecked eyes of the social rebel were doubtless flashing. 'You're always bending the knee to the gentry. *I* say that Miss Jenny is one of the cas-u-al- ities of the sex war.'

Jim's long fingers clutched the banister. It was one thing to take a chance on a relatively small matter like Jenny's malaise not reaching his mother's ears. But this! It would be swept up the hillside tomorrow morning on an irresistible wave of charwomen ascending to the mansions and mini-mansions of Upper Glenmorris. There, after a preliminary snub from their mistresses, they would be allowed to advance their proofs. The news would be spread by their mistresses over the clinking of teacups, more respectably — more dangerously. His mother of course would be the last to hear. But it needed only one malicious tongue . . . His mother might put this together with the sudden plans for sending Jenny to London. She might question his father.

''Tis a nasty thing to say.' The voice was Mrs O'Donovan's. 'Why don't you think before you speak?'

'Before I say anything nasty, I do always count to ten. Gives me time to think of something nastier.'

Mrs O'Donovan played her trump card. 'If Miss Jenny's in trouble, then what man? Sure, there's no man.'

'There's Mister Jim.'

Jim's fingers on the banister relaxed. Let their speculation range in that direction as far as they wished.

'Wouldn't it give you the sick to hear you!' Mrs O'Donovan's voice had risen.

'Mister Jim's *father*,' slipped in Eileen O'Herliky slyly, 'seems very fond of her. I've watched them crossing the hall here.'

The knuckles of the hand holding the banister blanched again. If she had noticed so much, wouldn't others have noticed sufficient to accept the possibility too? If the scent were not to lead the baying pack in the right direction, then a false one must be laid across it, and laid across it at once.

The sliding panel of the opening through which callers were interviewed had, unauthorised, been closed, doubtless to give privacy to the conversation within. As Jim quietly drew it back, Mrs O'Donovan was shaking her steel coils. 'The cheek of you, to be saying a thing the like o' that!'

'You've plenty of cheek yourself. You've two on your face, and two flingin' out behind.'

'You're rude and vulgar.'

The receptionist, seated on her high stool, her snowy elbows leaning on the counter within the sliding panel, started round as the lean tall figure poised over her as though about to swoop. It helped not at all that he was smiling. She nibbled at her red-varnished nails.

He looked into the red-brown eyes raised to him. He had hitherto regarded her as a good-natured blarneying girl rather than this sharp miss. 'You ought to be a detective. Every detective likes to know if he has succeeded. Well now, Miss Jenny doesn't have many close men friends. I think I've been around her a lot of her life. And I'm very fond of babies.' His smile became broader. 'I hope to have dozens.' He glanced at his watch. 'Well, must get back to my desk. Increasing family responsibilities, you know!'

He closed the panel quietly. As he returned upstairs, he heard Eileen O'Herlihy gasp, 'God, isn't that a fright?' Then came Mrs O'Donovan's, 'Think o' that, now!'

Henry, back in his office, was bent over the long high desk. He held the make-up that he was examining with Mr Quin, the head printer. 'Now, when *I* was a boy —' He refrained from glancing round as his son passed. But he had heard the voices in the foyer, and something in their tones had made him uneasy.

Jim lowered his long form on to his swing seat. He smiled grimly. How he had silenced the barn fowl! How he had outraged every second-hand idea in the spruce little repositories of their minds! How he had slapped aside the chief of their Commandments: thou shalt do thy best to hush it up! In lieu of paste, he pinned his drawing by its edge into place in the general design.

He was too restless to concentrate. As he made his way to Jenny, he became aware that his father was ending his conference. Jim tapped on her door. 'You wanted to tell your mother that you're going to have a baby. Well, you can. If you don't, the rest of Glenmorris may.' He gave her the story, suppressing only the reference to his father.

'Now,' said his father's voice, 'you've raised the matter from rumour to apparent fact.' The listening Henry stood in the doorway. 'Your mother will have to be told.'

Jim swung round. 'No!'

'Sooner or later someone will ask her when Jenny and you are going to get married. We can't let her find out like that.'

Jim darted a startled look at Henry; desperation had lifted his father out of his lethargy. But he still replied doggedly, 'Who cares what this one-horse little town thinks?'

'Your mother has to. It's her world.'

Jim looked more closely at the deep-set eyes under the heavy brows. Besides the fever that burned in them, there was devotion.

Jenny rose with quick grace from her desk. 'Jim, you can't lumber yourself with this. I'll say it's someone I met in Cork.'

Henry watched the vigorous shake of his son's head. 'No good! Must be something instantly believed.'

Henry chilled. 'Why shouldn't Jenny have met someone in Cork?'

Jim's voice was the more ominous for being hardly above a whisper. 'The hounds are within half an inch of baying down the right trail.' He revealed Eileen O'Herlihy's guess. 'That I won't allow. We must call off the London visit. We — we must get married.'

Jenny regarded him. Married to Jim! There would be two people, when the baby arrived, for her to look after. Assertion over the baby and surrender to Jim . . . She shook herself. 'I'll say I refused to marry you with a pistol to your head.'

Henry observed his son pause. He was considering this. Well, the boy couldn't be blamed. But Jenny was looking crestfallen.

Jim seemed to have noticed. 'It's just that I resent being drawn into what amounts to a conspiracy against my mother.'

'Jim, there are no sides.' It came almost as a cry from Henry. 'I'm disgusted with myself.'

He heard Jenny put in quickly, '*We* are disgusted with ourselves.'

'What happened to you might happen to anybody.' His son's voice had lost some of its bitterness. 'We'll be married in a registry office.' Bitterness returned. 'I'll not go into a church.'

Henry opened his mouth, then closed it again. Unaccustomed situation, to be controlled by others instead of controlling them! How the boy was taking over, and at what a price!

Jenny spoke. 'I wouldn't want it in a church myself.'

Was there a doubt in her voice? She would feel awkward with the padre; apart from meetings at Sunday services, she still crewed for him in the weekend yacht races held in the harbour.

Because of his anxiety, Henry scarcely noticed in the flash of his headlights the flaking plaster and chipped paint of the Byrnes' house, the roof of which still had not had the promised attention of Mason, that almost mythical workman. He pulled on the handbrake. A moment later he was round the bonnet and handing out Jenny respectfully. It was the moment of her confession to her mother.

'Will you be all right?'

'Yes.' Her voice was sharp. 'Why not?' As he had driven along, he had been aware of her nibbling at her nails; she was always most gallant when she was most afraid.

If Henry's gaze could have followed her through that front door as it closed behind her, he would have seen a further hardening in that usually friendly, sometimes troubled, face. She found her mother over her game of Patience at the corner of the dining-room table nearest the fire. Jenny flopped down into the facing armchair that had been her father's.

'I'm going to have a baby.'

Mildred extracted herself out of her cards. '*What's* that you said?'

'I'm going to have a baby.' She added with greater difficulty, 'It's Jim's.'

Mildred raised her bangled wrists in conventional horror and secret delight. But she couldn't restrain a skittish laugh. 'You young people nowadays! Well, I don't know!' She fondled the dog on her lap. So now all was explained; Jenny's food fancies, the rush to get her to London! The rush to get her to London . . . Did that mean that Jim wasn't going to . . . 'When have you arranged to get married?'

'What's the hurry?'

'Hurry! Of course there's a hurry. What's Canon Moss going to say if you don't hurry? What's Henry going to say? Doesn't Jim want to hurry?'

'All these men! Who made them rulers over women?'

Mildred ceased mechanically fondling the dog. 'The women will think the same. Don't you think the same?'

78

Jenny flushed. 'I won't eat humble pie any longer. I've wanted a baby since my first doll.'

'It's one thing to have a baby. It's another to have a —'

Jenny jumped to her feet. 'To have what?'

The dog arose also, leapt out of Mildred's lap, and took refuge under her skirt.

'Dear, you *know* what I mean. I'll use no unkind word. But facts are facts. If you don't marry, it will be a future of struggle that will lie before you.'

'When you have somebody depending on you, there's nothing you can't do.' She sat down again. 'I'm a fully qualified secretary.'

'What about your confinement?'

Jenny's eyes were fixed on the jumping flames, the light flickering over her blonde hair. Her baby would be frail at first. She would nurse him through that. He would grow up to be more powerful than herself; be all the things she couldn't be.

'What about your confinement? Your father didn't leave me much.'

'All right, Mummy. Jim's going to marry me.'

Mildren dropped her hands into her lap with a jingle of relief. The dog emerged and, deciding that there was to be no battle, jumped back into his place. Mildred reflected that she would be able to re-live her life through her daughter and the baby. There was Jim himself; undoubtedly he was attracted to her in some unacknowledged corner of his heart. She had often caught his blue eyes fixed on her cheeks; doubtless he was fascinated by her milkmaid complexion. What must Henry have thought of her remark about not letting Jenny get into trouble through keeping the wrong company! 'I wonder what Vera will say.'

Yes, Vera . . . Jenny stared into the fire. *She* couldn't be shuffled away into the managing world of men and the gossiping world of women and there defied — Vera, loving, dignified, betrayed.

The flicking of the Patience cards, as they once more began to be deposited on the table first here then there, became slower then finally ceased. There was that occasion two years ago . . . Jenny, for ever dreaming of motherhood, had somehow got hold of a medical book. Mildred had found it on her dressing-table. She had flicked over the pages. Horrified by the explicit photographs, she had silently confiscated it. Jenny had remained silent also . . .

Henry drove on, unaccustomedly slouched over the wheel. His face was set in an expression of pain. The truth had kept bursting out, like a sea that would not be denied by the dykes that had been hastily reared to contain it. The very devotion with which the boy had attempted to plug the torrent only added to his shame. They were doing all the lying for him, while he sheltered behind their embarrassments. He had no right to accept this marriage. Yet to reject it was worse.

His son's voice came from the back of the car. 'Dad, please drop me off at the rectory. I'm letting the padre know that we're being married in a registry office. I don't want just to go over his head.'

Henry gave his sharp nod, but his fingers tightened on the wheel. When *he* was a boy, nobody would have thought of such a thing. What could he say? Goodness knew, he had no right to speak. Ahead, he made out the square bell-tower of St Patrick's Church. Wasn't the true position, that he had no right *not* to speak? Perhaps God would count it in his favour that he had made a stand from a position of such appalling weakness. 'Jim, you ought to be married in the Church of your Fathers.'

'It may be the Church of my Fathers, but it certainly isn't mine.'

Henry's lip twitched. 'Tch! I don't know what Canon Moss will say.'

'There's a light in the church.'

A rook, perched by the Hampton vault, was reading the inscription with grave biscuit-beaked attention. The old tower hovered ponderously in the indigo sky. Bats hurried out of the shuttered vents, then flitted in again. A cat peered upwards in puzzlement, regarding them as mice that had been unfairly equipped by nature. The organ hummed from the sad evening building, its gravestones standing about it like sentinels. The moan of Masterman floated in on the salt air, and moved over the churchyard like a melancholy poltergeist.

Inside the edifice, Henry's eye fell on a group gathered round the green and white marble font. He entered a pew and sank to his knees. His son joined him.

Canon Moss, when reading prayers, had a habit of looking away from the text as though to see how much he could repeat by heart. 'Dearly beloved,' he was saying, flicking the end of the black ribbon that served as a marker in his prayer-book so that it swung to and fro, 'forasmuch as all men are conceived and born in sin; and that our Saviour Christ saith' — he became apparently deeply interested in a beetle crawling over the foot of the font — 'none can enter into the kingdom of God, except he be regenerate and born anew of Water and of the Holy Ghost' — Canon Moss sucked his teeth thoughtfully, staring up at an electric light — 'I beseech you to call upon God the Father — upon,' repeated Canon Moss uncertainly, 'God the father' — he searched the open page before him frantically — 'God the father' — he discovered the place and, with a new-found burst of confidence, continued on safely to the end.

Henry particularly disapproved of the padre's habit of joining in the last few words of the responses, and even in the whole of them.

Canon Moss, to give variety to the service, suddenly changed into his high wail. 'Dost thou believe,' he said, addressing himself to the god-parents, 'in the resurrection of the flesh, and everlasting life after death?'

'All this I steadfastly believe,' muttered the god-parents.

'— steadfastly believe,' said Canon Moss.

'Wilt thou,' demanded Canon Mass, 'be baptised in this faith?'

'That is my desire,' said the god-parents *sotto voce*.

'That is my desire,' echoed Canon Moss.

The baby duly baptised, he passed it back to the godmother. 'And now, my friends, a prayer for your safe journey to Australia. Let us kneel.'

'Amen,' said Canon Moss, as he misconcluded the final prayer. Pressing with his hand on one knee, he half jerked up his heavy body. 'Amen,' he grunted. He clutched at the edge of the font, like a drowning man grasping *terra firma*. 'Amen,' he groaned. He got himself up. 'Amen, amen,' he sighed in relief and satisfaction.

Jim's right ear became conscious of that low growl which was his father's best approach to a whisper. 'Did you notice the way he had to ketch on to the font? He oughtn't to be working.'

As the baptismal group departed, Henry advanced, his son following. 'You look tired, Padre. You ought to retire.'

Canon Moss gave his thin laugh. 'We'd have to be dropping before the Church of Ireland could afford to retire us.'

'We must see if we ken't set you up a retirement fund. Er — Jim wants to speak to you. I'll wait in the car.' And Henry was striding out of the church.

The padre's small grey eyes under their wild eyebrows followed him. Long time since Hampton had given him a frying for — borrowing — from Church funds for his little unauthorised charities . . . 'Come into the vestry, Jim.' He divested himself of his outer robes as he went. 'Sit down. Sit down.'

Jim remained standing, his legs apart, his thumbs thrust into the pockets of an orange-brown waistcoat in soft leather. 'Padre, Jenny and I are being married in a registry office.'

Placing a hairy paw on each arm of his ecclesiastical chair, Canon Moss, still garbed in his long black cassock, lowered his huge expanse of chest and stomach. From the betasselled velvet-topped table beside him he picked up his pipe. This he placed in the side of his mouth, in the convenient space formed by the missing tooth.

'Once knew a fellah, Jim —' Because of the need to clench his pipe, his voice emerged muffled. He reached for his pouch and shook flakes of tobacco into his cupped palm. 'Once knew a fellah whose wife gave birth to twins whom he knew weren't his. At first he was bitter. But when later the twins held up their arms to him' — he ground up the tobacco, using the square top of one finger as the pestle in the mortar of his palm — 'as he came in the morning to lift them out of their cot, he said they became his, because they made him theirs.' Extracting the pipe from his mouth, Canon Moss seemed absorbed in using the same finger to pack down the tobacco into the bowl. 'No smear is proof against a baby's trust and love; every child is a purge and a new beginning. Whether I say the words or not, he is born anew of Water and of the Holy Ghost.'

So the padre knew he was not the father! Jim sharply surveyed the folds and creases of Canon Moss's visage. Did he know who was?

The padre began to suck in and shoot out his thick lips. His aggressive jaw moved in and out like a piston. 'I think Jenny believes in God.' He darted out his tongue at Jim, only to snap it back into

82

his mouth again. The next moment all the aggression was being dissipated in the high thin laugh.

The thumbs were thrust deeper into the waistcoat pockets. 'Jenny said she didn't want a church ceremony either.'

Canon Moss's features resumed working in a series of expressions of good-humoured pugnacity. 'Did she mean it? Supreme moment in a woman's life. Can't ever be replaced later.'

Abruptly Jim sat down. He crossed his long legs. 'Padre, I've no hostility towards the Church. Rather, I've an affection for it. But it's one thing to be a sympathetic, occasionally amused, bystander. It's another to act as a principal in one of its ceremonies.'

The padre, whose eyebrows had lifted momentarily at the word 'amused', recovered his balance. 'Yes, yes, Jim,' he trumpeted. 'I get you, I get you.' His pale eyes rolled reflectively up to the vestry ceiling, so that the whites showed below. 'Of course,' he said slowly, his fingers rubbing in his cropped scant grey hair, 'the ceremony could be quite private. You'd be surrounded by just a few of the people closest to you.'

Jim tapped one of the tassels of the velvet-topped table. He watched it swinging. He saw his mother's saddened face when he announced, together with his paternity, his refusal to be wed in a church. 'All right, padre.'

Canon Moss's eyes descended again. The creases and folds of his visage shone. 'You could be married almost at once by special licence.'

There was a vigorous shake of the young head. 'No, Padre, I won't pay that homage to the gossips. We'll be married after the usual lapse of time.'

Canon Moss's jaw worked for a moment, then subsided. Enough was enough.

If he wasn't being logical, Jim reflected as he closed the vestry outside door behind him, in making a number of vows in the name of a god in whose existence he didn't believe , neither were they in accepting them from him.

Henry, on hearing of the outcome from Jim, gave his double nod. 'Why don't Jenny and you go to London for an art course after the wedding? Get you out of the gossip.'

'No thank you, Dad.'

Henry pressed his lips together. The boy wasn't going to accept payment for having his married life messed up. It was the second twisting of the knife in Henry's side. The first was when he had set down Jenny at her door. But he didn't succumb — yet.

When they reached Karachi House it was to encounter the missionary, his pince-nez pinching his nose and winking, arrived ahead of time and with an unexpected wife. He turned out to possess one of those perfectly round faces peculiar to men who combine a deep religious conviction with an addiction to pickled gherkins. Vera, looking gracious and distinguished, a beaded gauze over her rich hair, introduced them.

At dinner, Henry watched his son sipping his French wine and eating little.

After coffee, the missionary arose. 'Well, my wife must go and play your excellent piano and practise her hymns, and I must go and play on my typewriter and practise my sermon.' All his life he had been an exceedingly witty man; he had made this joke (his only one) regularly for the past thirty years.

Henry rose too. 'I'll open the piano for you.' Leaving the room with his visitors, he was aware of his son's eyes on him.

As Jim proceeded to make his 'confession' in a tone both mechanical and bitter, he suddenly became aware that his mother was not so much listening to him as looking at him. Had her perception of character pierced through the artificiality of his contrition? Though now sharply alerted to the danger, he found himself barren of further words.

He finished lamely, 'I'm sorry you should have been troubled with all this.'

'There's no need for you to be sorry, darling. Jenny's a delightful girl.'

'I'll make my way down to the studio.'

She linked her arm in his as they walked to the door. 'It's a good match.' She added quietly, 'If you *are* the father.'

He turned a white face. 'Yes. Yes, I'm the father.'

She looked at him, then smiled gently.

Opening the door, they found Henry apparently searching for something in the drawer of the hall-stand. *Christians Awake* on the piano floated through the drawing-room door. The gospel message rat-tatted down the staircase from the missionary's bedroom.

'I'm just seeing Jim off to the studio,' said Vera.

Henry's glance flitted from one strained face to the other. 'Yes.' He closed the drawer. 'I'll drive you down, Jim.'

'I prefer to cycle. I'll use that old bicycle in the garage.'

'Keep you company.' He moved determinedly to his son's side. 'Just as far as the gate.' Half way down the drive he blurted out, 'It's up to me to take on the onus, Jim. I won't tell your mother until after Jenny and you have left for London.'

'No, Dad. Certainly not. Just think how Jenny would feel even at a distance! Appearing like that before someone who's almost a second mother! They'll have to meet again some time. It's more than Mother should be called on to bear.'

He mounted the bicycle. As he cycled along slowly under the few lights of the quay, a flock of swans swam past, white-arched serenity slipping by. Peace hovered over the shabby beautiful little town. He overtook two countrywomen wearing the heavy black cloaks of the district. The squeaking of the old bicycle made them turn their heads. Their faces, white against the surrounding dark material, peered out at him from the voluminous hoods. Was there an added curiosity in their eyes? Had Eileen O'Herlihy already spread her tale? The swans dropped away down the harbour and were lost in the night.

Over the click of her needles Vera said, 'Henry, you weren't too hard on Jim over this — this . . . He seems bitter.'

Ten minutes before, the missionary, smiling his dreadful smile (he had a good heart but bad teeth), had departed with his wife to bed.

'No, no.' Henry rose abruptly and rearranged the fire with the long brass poker. 'Must lock up the greenhouse.'

'You've borne a great deal of worry, old boy. I know you're just trying to save me, but I do like to help.'

Henry put down the poker. He gave his double nod. 'Must lock up the greenhouse,' he muttered to the mantlepiece.

Out on the drive the night air cooled his brow. The missionary was standing by his bedroom window examining the heavens. In his hands he clutched one of those greenish hot-water bottles so beloved of Methodist ministers with unacknowledged Unitarian leanings.

Jim's refusal to allow himself to be driven down to the studio had been the third twisting of the knife — and the last.

Chapter Seven

It was on the night of the following day that Henry did not sleep at all. The missionary had left, taking with him his wife and his ledger. In this ledger he kept statistics of the numbers he had baptised year by year. There were even graphs. These showed a satisfactory growth in the rate at which he was getting souls into heaven. Jim had speculated as to whether the Almighty paid him a bounty at so much a head.

As Henry stared at the dim ceiling of his bedroom, he saw clearly the hand of God in the trials that were being inflicted on Jim. God was scourging him, Henry, by causing him to bedevil the life of one of the three beings, Vera, Jenny, his son, whom he most wished to serve. He could no longer simply believe that God's laws were as they were, because to disregard them brought an automatic evil; that God had set his universe running, and had then with- drawn his intervention. Was it not written in the bible, 'Are not two sparrows sold for a farthing? and one of them shall not fall to the ground without your Father. But the very hairs of your head are numbered. Fear ye not therefore, ye are of more value than many sparrows.' So nothing was set running! God came down minute by minute into the life of each individual. He, Henry, had prayed that, if it were God's will, his deed should not bring unhappiness on those he had wronged. But it had *not* been God's will. Jenny, against all the odds, had become pregnant. Jenny's and his plans to keep her pregnancy secret had not been allowed either. The truth had broken through not only to Jim, to Vera, to Mildred, but, via perhaps some at the printing works, to the whole town.

No, it was more than a scourging. God was destroying him; had decided upon his destruction. Without disturbing Vera, he descended to his study. There he wrote steadily for an hour before returning.

In the morning, Vera took one look at him and sent for Dr O'Grady. That Henry agreed to see him was part of his increased gentleness towards her. Dr O'Grady examined him at length, stroked his long grey beard, screwed up his nose, blew out his cheeks, and prescribed bed and a sedative.

Suddenly Henry spoke. 'Doctor, is it likely that a woman would become pregnant after a single — occasion?'

As usual, Doctor O'Grady first sought a second opinion from the ceiling. 'Rather improbable. There are a number of factors that have to be right at the same time. What's brought this on?'

'Just — a parish problem that the padre and I have to sort out.' Moral lisping again! 'Are there difficulties in diagnosing pregnancy?'

'Not usually. There's little doubt about it when a young woman has missed several periods, has morning sickness, tenderness of the breasts, and has been leading a normal sex life.'

'Normal! One — occasion — is hardly normal.'

'No. No, I suppose not.' Dr O'Grady threaded his fingers through his beard. 'Has she had a pregnancy test? They're over ninety per cent accurate.'

'I believe not. When would a diagnosis be a hundred per cent accurate?'

'The foetal heartbeat. You can hear it with a stethoscope after four months or so.'

'I see. I'll mention it to the padre.' Tenderness of the breast! It fitted.

The sound of Dr O'Grady's trap had hardly died away upon the drive, when Henry arose.

'Now, old boy, do stop in bed.'

'Ah, for goodness sake, woman . . .' He leant towards her dressing-table mirror, knotting his tie meticulously. 'I must get to church. I want to see Jim.' He picked up a sheaf of papers.

The stride that took him to his car was feverish rather than brisk, as though the ticking away of time on the gold fob-watch in his pocket had suddenly speeded up. Vera followed him.

Jim, who attended church for his mother's sake, was already in the family pew. He rose to allow his mother to pass beyond him, then sat down again. Henry took his seat beside him at the end nearer the aisle. It was the end, all the way down the church, occupied

88

by the eldest male. The younger males were ranged within. Inside this protective barrier, presumably against any stray wolves or other predators which might happen to be roaming the aisle, sat the women and children.

Canon Moss's boots resounded on the chancel tiles as he emerged from the vestry to lead the service. His bullet head was covered by tufts of greyish-brown hair, looking like dried-up grass. This bullet head, and his thick neck, gave him something of the aspect of a bison, as far as its air of solid aggressiveness was concerned. Before one Harvest Thanksgiving service an over-enthusiastic lady, assisting in the decoration of the church, had surrounded and smothered the padre's seat with a mass of flowers, branches of greenery, and sheaves of corn. In the midst of the service the congregation had been startled to hear a sudden crashing, as of a heavy animal plunging through undergrowth. It was the padre, emerging from the jungle round his seat on his way to the sanctuary to read the Commandments.

Canon Moss always conducted the service with an air of bluff casualness that, together with the regimental badge on his stole, dating from the days when he had been padre to the British troops in King William Fort, suggested a colonel talking to his officers.

'If we say that we have no sin, we deceive ourselves,' said Canon Moss in a bluff conversational tone, 'and the truth is not in us.' He rocked himself back and forth on his heels and toes and gazed up at the ceiling, as though planning military manoeuvres.

'Dearly beloved brethren,' said Canon Moss, 'the scripture moveth us in sundry places to acknowledge and confess our manifold sins and wickedness' — he gazed out through one of the mullioned windows high up in the wall opposite him, with a far-away look, giving the impression that his thoughts were on the success of his winter lettuce.

He descended on to his knees, and was followed by the congregation. Opposite him, across the chancel, was the little sprinkling of the choir, the organ behind them. As he prayed, he kept jutting out his jaw at them in the most menacing way as though they had incurred his wrath, but the next moment the jaw would withdraw itself somewhat, and his mouth would widen until it seemed to be smiling in some secret amusement.

'Almighty and most merciful Father, we have erred and strayed from thy ways like lost sheep.' Canon Moss thrust out his jaw and glared at a woman with a huge red face, a big blunt-ended nose, and a hat like a small dish. 'We have followed too much the devices and desires of our own hearts.' He grinned secretly, as though contemplating some devilish pranks of his own.

'I believe,' cried Canon Moss a little later, 'in God the Father Almighty, maker of heaven and earth . . .'

He stood in a peculiar attitude in his pew. This attitude was a compromise between facing the Communion Table, and facing the choir. Two forces moved the padre. On the one hand were nostalgic memories of conducting high-church Anglican services for the British troops where, during the recital of the Creed, all not already doing so would turn to face the Communion table. On the other hand there was deference to his present Church of Ireland congregation. All the choir presented sturdy low-church profiles to those in the body of the building. Thus, by refraining from turning themselves towards the Communion Table, they avoided the appearance of praying to an altar, or to a figure in stained glass or carving, or any similar idolatrous practice such as was found, it was alleged, among Catholics and all similarly deluded persons.

The pulpit, only a wooden structure, trembled as the padre's fifteen stone ascended the steps. 'For unto everyone that hath shall be given,' said Canon Moss, announcing his text, 'and he shall have abundance; but from him that hath not shall be taken away even that which he hath.'

He paused, while the obscurities and paradoxes of this utterance soaked into the pates of his hearers. He gathered his forces to deal with the facer he had set himself. A look of cogitation involved his mobile features. His light grey eyes, in the midst of the fiery brick-red face, rolled up to the ceiling and his mouth opened wide as though gasping for air. He appeared to be on the point of collapse after a surfeit of alcohol.

Henry's hoarse *sotto voce*, his nearest approach to a whisper, sounded in his son's right ear. 'I've some papers for you, Jim. I'm putting them down on the seat beside you. Don't tell your mother.'

Canon Moss had resumed. His eyes still on the ceiling, his mouth, as he spoke slowly and reflectively, opening very wide so that he looked like one of the mackerel snapping after his own spinning-bait, he changed into his higher voice. 'What — is — the — meaning — of — this — saying?'

The congregation cudgelled its brains, was blessed if it knew, and hoped a little anxiously that the padre did.

Henry's *sotto voce* was back. 'They set out the whole workings of the business. If anything happened to me, you'd have to take over. Mr Sparrow and Mr Quinn, of course —'

'Let me paraphrase it for you,' continued Canon Moss in his high thin voice. 'Suppose I were to say, "Don't use, and lose; use, and gain."' On the word 'gain', he descended into his baritone.

The congregation was no clearer than it had been before.

Jim's startled blue eyes were on his father. 'Come off it, Dad! Nothing's going to happen to you.'

'Let me,' said Canon Moss, 'give you an example. When we were children, we learnt with ease dates and pieces of poetry. Now, fifty years on,' (Canon Moss apparently considered his entire audience to be more or less his own age) 'our schooldays are past, no need to learn such things, and as a consequence we should find it very hard to do so. When we use our memories, we increase their power. When we cease to use them, we lose them. Don't use, and lose. Use, and gain. Unto everyone that hath shall be given, but from him that hath not shall be taken away even that which he hath.'

There followed a pause to allow the congregation, and Canon Moss, to admire the ingeniousness of the explanation. Henry used it to growl, 'Just read the papers later, Jim.' His lip twitched.

Greatly delighted with himself, Canon Moss set himself to his task anew. 'Let me give you another example. We thought nothing of walking five, seven, even ten miles. But the young people nowadays, since the proliferation of the motor-car, groan if they have to walk two miles. Use your legs, and what happens? What happens?' He gazed around, as though he expected someone to rise out of his pew and furnish him with a reply. 'Why,' said Canon Moss triumphantly, 'your legs get stronger. And if you don't use them, what happens? What happens? Why,' cried Canon Moss, 'they become weaker. Don't use, and lose. Use, and gain.'

A movement of satisfaction passed over the congregation. They felt relieved and delighted that the matter had been cleared up. This relief was marred for the younger generation by their being represented as almost limbless products of the age of the internal combustion engine, in contrast with their sturdy forbears. The younger members invariably came off second best in the padre's comparisons.

There followed another pregnant pause while Canon Moss gathered his forces. Henry noticed Vera peering round from her position beyond Jim. He relaxed as the boy slipped the papers into his nearer pocket.

'You may say to yourself that you can't do much,' said Canon Moss, 'and that therefore it is not worth doing anything. But wait. Have you ever dropped a stone into a pool? Have you?'

Jim momentarily forgot his uneasiness. Surely the padre wasn't going to trot out that ancient one about the ripples travelling out in ever widening circles!

'It makes only a little splash perhaps,' said Canon Moss, 'and the splash is followed perhaps by only a few circles on the surface of the water. *But,*' said Canon Moss, turning on the full power of his baritone, so that it rang through the church like a heavenly fanfare, 'those small circles will spread out ever wider until at last they reach the limits of the pool. So,' said Canon Moss, 'if you do what you can, however little it may be, by divers unsuspected ways that little may — who knows, who knows? — come to make its impulses felt throughout the whole community. And then shall Gard' — Canon Moss's accent, which outside his church was that of an ordinary educated man who had spent the greater part of his life in the County Cork, in the pulpit assumed from time to time the most extraordinary guises — 'and then shall Gard say to you, "Enter thou into the jy of thy Lee-ud." '

In the concluding hymn, the choir gave of their best.

'The rich man in his castle,
The poor man at his gate,
God made them high or lowly,
And ordered their estate.'

Upper Glenmorris had no doubt of it.

On his way round the church to the outside door into the vestry, Henry observed a pram. In the pram a baby lay kicking with a hectic expression on its face. Beyond it, in the middle distance, stood

Mildred Byrne. She frisked towards him, moving her hands in a gesture of flirtatious greeting; her shoes, very high-heeled to show off her racehorse ankles, scattered the gravel.

'And when's the wedding date?' She put on a gay laugh.

'After the usual interval of time,' said Henry shortly.

He knocked on the vestry door. A moment later he escaped through it out of her bangled chatter. The baby, now with a round comforter stuck into its round face, watched her with round eyes.

The Canon was poring over the table upon whose red velvet top lay the notes and coins of the collection. 'Er, let me see . . .' His thick lips sucked in and shot out. 'Two shillings and eight pence, and seven pence, make three and five —'

'Three and three, surely,' interjected Henry. 'Shall I give you a hand?'

'Do, do.' He had twice been through the collection, and the two resulting totals had varied from one another to quite an astonishing degree. 'Excellent congregation, eh, Hampton! About a hundred and twenty people, I reckon from the collection.'

'I made it ninety-eight.' Henry's square fingers herded together the half crowns, florins, shillings and sixpences, and the pennies of the children. 'You ken't really tell the number from counting the number of coins. I mean to say, one person might put in several.' He jotted down the total. 'I think, Padre, you'd better make arrangements today for someone to take over my jobs.' Canon Moss appeared to be making no efforts to replace him.

'You're the best man for the job, Hampton.'

'I'm sorry. There — are private reasons.'

'You don't think yourself worthy?' Henry's startled glance was met by the padre's steady grey eyes. 'Don't forget St Peter. Denied his Lord. Lived to be the rock on which the Church was founded.'

The lines on Henry's still strong face were deeper. 'Padre —' But he closed his lips again.

'You know the wonderful language of our Communion Service, "Hear what comfortable words our Saviour Christ saith unto all that truly turn to him: come unto me all that travail and are heavy laden, and I will refresh you." ' On this occasion the good Canon's memory didn't fail him. ' "Hear also what St John saith: if any man

93

sin, we have an advocate with the Father, Jesus Christ the righteous, and he is the propitiation for our sins." '

Some of the fever left Henry's eyes. He gave his double nod. 'Well, I must be getting along.'

The padre moved beside him to the door. 'You couldn't make your wife happier than just by letting her see that you are your old self again.'

'It wasn't much of an old self.'

'Oh, not bad at all!' trumpeted Canon Moss. 'Not bad at all!'

So the padre knew! It was a relief. Henry, his face averted, his bearded cheeks wet, walked away quickly. On his way to join Vera in the car, he paused before the family vault. His great uncle Albert, a suicide it was whispered, was not buried there . . . The baby, now removed from its pram and with its cheek held against its mother's, was observing the crazy world about it with a distracted expression.

Canon Moss, still at the outer vestry door, spotted Dr O'Grady chatting on the drive. 'Can you spare me a moment?'

The long grey beard approached. 'Certainly.'

'Doctor, shall have to be a bit mysterious. Sit down, sit down!' He closed the door. 'Delicate matter. Involves a male parishioner. Can't help it if perhaps you guess.'

'I'll keep my guesses to myself, Padre.'

'Question is, in a phantom pregnancy, how far can matters go? Could an experienced — observer — be deceived?'

'All the way. Or nearly all the way. Women with an intense desire to be pregnant, or an intense fear of being pregnant, have felt a non-existent baby moving about. They can even experience labour pains.'

'I see. I see.'

Dr O'Grady consulted the vestry ceiling. Why should the padre have expected him to guess? Plainly it was the unnamed parishioner, or the woman associated with him, whom Henry had earlier had in mind. 'A pregnancy test of course would show that there was nothing there.'

'Quite. Perhaps we shall have to arrange for that.'

'The whole thing is in the mind. Treatment has to be by psychotherapy.'

*   *   *

94

After lunch, and by way of a constitutional, Henry walked down to the town. He hoped to collect a shirt which was having a new collar and new cuffs put on it. The tailor was a man with a face like a sponge; it soaked up instructions with a glistening eagerness. Henry particularly disliked the way he slid his soap-like hands round one's own, holding them clammily while he received his orders.

On his way out of Karachi House, Henry had passed through the kitchen. Bridie was full of gruesome news and therefore of gusto. "Tis no luck at all they're having with that young fellah. Evening after evening they're dragging for him. They've brought up bits of the boat, and his jacket; everything except hisself.'

Henry, at the sink, continued to remove some grease from his hands. 'All right, Bridie!'

'Sure, he should never have gone out in that rotten old tub, with that weight o' sand in her. The bottom fell out of her.' The imbecile, it had been reported, could not swim. In addition he was wearing sea-boots, which must have filled at once. 'He was drownded, the creature.'

Henry turned his back more fully upon her. With cupped hands he passed cold water over his tall brow.

'Sure, the only thing to do is to wait twenty-one days till he floats again.'

'All right, Bridie! All right!' He dried his face and hands on the roller towel.

'If ye ask me, 'tis that cat there that art to be drownded.' She regarded pussy, curled up by the range, with a hostile eye. 'Ach, yer dirty mangy brute!'

'No,' he had snapped. 'If she's to be put down, it must be done properly by the vet. Her kitten it still too young to be alone.'

He had left the kitchen and made his way down the hill. Cows surveyed him soulfully over a gate, munching.

Canon Moss had sat over his Sunday lunch ill at ease. After what he had just learned from Dr O'Grady, he couldn't let matters drift. But whom to see first, Henry or Jenny? Of the two, Jenny had appeared to be much the more secure. Sometimes it almost seemed as though she wanted the baby, that is, if there was a baby. No, his greatest source of unease was Henry. The rigidity of Henry's mind, of his beliefs, was his strength, and also his weakness.

Presently the antiquated grey Morris-Cowley lumbered down the rectory drive. Passing the back entrance to Karachi House on his way round to the front, he saw Bridie disposing of some rubbish into a bin.

'Is the master at home, Bridie?'

'Himself is after goin' into the town, sir.'

'D'you know where?'

'No, I don't rightly know, sir.'

'Thank you.'

The Morris made its way down the hill. Bridie having failed to mention that Henry had walked, and the padre to remember that he was by no means a limbless member of the age of the internal combustion engine, it was for a shiny black limousine, moving or parked, that the few streets of the sleepy little town were explored.

Henry stood in front of a door with a knocker. It wasn't much of a knocker. The metal stud, upon which it was supposed to strike, was misplaced, and the knocker struck the wood of the door with a dull thud. Quite a pit had been worn.

'The tailor's out, sir.' The voice came from the roadway behind him. He turned and saw a woman dressed in her shabby Sunday best. 'He's gone down to Prescott's for his paper. He's gone for *The People*.'

He stared at her. So she not only knew that the tailor was out, but where he had gone, why he had gone there, and even the name of the paper he read! The full force of small-town curiosity, of its thirst after its neighbour's doings, its famine-hunger to know them in all their minutiae, hit him like a terror. The woman's bony face, her eyes and her mouth agape and alight, gazed back at him like a mask with a furnace of enquiry blazing behind it, burning to pluck his mind from him, his family's secrets, the scandals that surrounded his son. And it was he who had exposed Jim, due to go to the altar in only ten days' time in a hideous mock-marriage to a bride carrying his own father's child, to that terrible invigilation!

'Thank you,' he muttered, and strode home through streets that were windows that watched him, projecting shop signs that pointed at him like fingers, and a rising wind that whispered scandal in the doorways.

Back at Karachi House, his eyes fastened on the two bald spots on the cat's temples. He noted the lustreless eye, the dried-up thinning hair, the body that seemed to have shrunk. She was always poking her nose into garbage; had she poisoned herself? She broke into a long bout of wheezing. He wouldn't have her in the house another minute. She was a walking vessel of disease.

He went to an outhouse. He pulled a sack from a shelf and shook out the dust. He found a roll of cord, and tied a stone to it. Was the stone heavy enough? He tied on a second. He fetched out the cat and put her into the sack. The sack bulged out here and there as the animal explored for the exit, now closed with the other end of the cord. Slinging the burden over his shoulder, he took the stones in his free hand and made his way to the garage.

Feelings of guilt invaded his mind. He concentrated on the condition of the cat. The resultant wave of revulsion ousted all other emotions. Everything foul should be taken to the sea. The sea swallowed up all, even as it had swallowed up the fouled wits and leering face of the imbecile. All the world's debris should be taken to, and lost in, the bitter cleanliness of the sea.

His boat lay at her moorings. For convenience, he had moved them back up the harbour from the slipway to some stone steps ascending the side of the quay wall. As he bent to the oars, he noted the empty deck of the little trading schooner, and the three fishermen on the quay too intent on mending the tarry fishing-net to have eyes for him. When the quay and its wooden and corrugated-iron warehouses had fallen sufficiently far astern, he shipped his oars. The cat had not once cried out. He rose to his feet. He lifted the sack by its neck, and the stones with his other hand. The musty smell of the sacking, and its movement as the cat fumbled about, was nauseous to him. He held the sack well away from his legs. Waves of pity, at what awaited the helpless unsuspecting animal within, alternated with determination to be rid of it. The weight of the stones was reassuring.

His heart fluttered as he poised himself in the stern. The strength drained from his hands. He swung back the sack. Pivoting at the waist, he hurled sack and stones from him. They hit the water together.

Horror! *The sack was floating.* It floated on the very surface, the air inside inflating it. Had nature suspended her laws; were the stones somewhere beneath the water floating too? Superstitious awe spurted through him. Hardly had it come, when the sack was whipped below the surface. One moment it was there; the next it was gone. He realised what had happened. Notwithstanding the weight of the stones, the comparative buoyancy conferred on them by the water had slowed down their rate of sinking. In addition, the length of cord to the sack was considerable. He stood staring at the grey moving water. Its pitiless indifferent surface might be tranquil but, down below, in what a mortal writhing of brain and muscle was a life being choked out.

Droplets glinted on his brow. It was he who was in the sack. He was hurtling through the air. There was a springy concussion. Water instantly began to come through the part of the sacking on which he was lying. Presently it was deep enough to swim in. There was still plenty of air. Abruptly some invisible hand was dragging him down. The water poured in through the interstices. The reservoir of air shrank upwards. He swam up with it. There was enough left only for his face. He stretched back his neck. The air was gone. He held the breath in his lungs, and tore at the walls of the chamber that was bearing him down to the harbour-fouled mud and the crabs. His nails were broken. Blood floated away from his finger tips. His head swam. Ah! God! The water rushed into his lungs . . .

He passed his hand over his brow. The masts and spars of the schooner seemed to shake in the Christmas-season sunshine. He grasped the oar handles, and the rowlocks began to knock to and fro in their holes.

He stood in the quay, looking out across the inner harbour. An aloof swan slid contemptuously by, white arched over grey. Suddenly a squally wind arose from nowhere. Blowing now from this direction, now from that, it painted the surface of the sea a darker grey with fierce impulsive brush-strokes. He himself was the foulest thing on the surface of the earth.

Chapter Eight

Canon Moss, having failed to make contact with Henry down in the town, directed the rounded brass top of the Morris-Cowley's radiator in the direction of Jenny's home. There he spent a considerable time.

Henry himself, back now again at Karachi House, tapped the barometer in the hall. The hand, already fallen sharply, fell yet further.

His eye alighted on Vera. She was sitting out in the garden in her overcoat. 'Ah, for goodness sake, woman! You'll ketch your death of cold.'

'Hello, darling!' She raised her head, a scarf tied over her hair. 'I was watching the clouds piling up. They make rather a noble sight, don't you think? By the way, have you seen the cat? The kitten has been mewing forlornly.'

His lip twitched. 'Tch,tch! What's this?' Tan-coloured topsails appeared above the promontory that divided the inner harbour from the outer. The next moment a magnificent three-masted schooner rounded the point. 'She's running in for shelter.' If others didn't do the same, there'd be more than cats drowned that night . . .

'I suppose, Henry, the motor-boat is big enough to ride out the storm. But hadn't you better bring in the rowing-boat?'

The rowing-boat! Yes, the rowing-boat . . . 'I'll be back in a moment.'

He extracted a parcel from a drawer in his study and returned. 'Ketch hold of this!'

'Oh, Henry, you remembered my birthday tomorrow!'

He joined her on the garden bench and watched her manicured fingers undo the wrappings. How old would she be? Forty-seven.

99

Himself fifty-three. Had she had a good life with him? Well, at least he had always loved her. She would know that.

'A prayer-book! You noticed that mine was falling to pieces. But what a beautiful one! It must have been very expensive.'

Yes, he hadn't shied away from the price. Something sacred to them both. Something to remember him by . . .

' "To my dearest wife." Old fellow, you couldn't have written anything nicer.' She put a hand on his shoulder and kissed him. 'Why did you give it to me the day before my birthday? You've never done that before.'

He kissed her too. His wife . . . The wife that God had given him . . . He rose. 'I must see to that boat.'

'Now, Henry, do be careful!' For a moment she considered adding: get Jim to give you a hand. But when had Henry ever neglected to conscript all the labour he could? 'Keep a look out for that cat!'

He gave his sharp double nod, and was gone.

The outside door of Dr O'Grady's surgery opened. Canon Moss and Jenny emerged from it on to the drive. Behind them the doctor's grey beard could be glimpsed for a moment before the door was closed again.

'Nothing to be down in the mouth about, young lady,' trumpeted the padre. 'Only nineteen. Plenty of time to have stacks of babies.'

The violet eyes, beneath their golden fringe, were rebellious. 'I'm fed up, Padre. Quite simply, I'm fed up.'

'I understand. But in all the circumstances —'

'Do you? Does any man? The baby's inside *me*. He goes to sleep, he wakes up, he moves around. I give him breath and food. He's my constant companion everywhere. We live together, we two, in a little universe of our very own. We have both long since put behind us how he got there. We pass no judgments on one another. It's enough for us that we both exist. He looks to me for life, and I to him for a reason to live. And now I'm told that he was never there at all; that my little companion was a mirage; that all this time I've been alone.' Tears pricked her eyes. Her cheeks burned.

Canon Moss spoke gently. 'I don't pass any judgments either. But the way is hard for an unmarried mother, especially in a small community.'

'I'd have gone away to Dublin. No, I'd have stayed and given Glenmorris as good as it gave.'

'Well, Jenny, we must get to Henry quickly. No longer the man he was. Afraid he's a man very ill in his mind.'

Her eyes turned sharply to the bulldog profile. Henry! Not Jim! Had the padre guessed? 'D'you think he's in some kind of danger?'

'Well, don't want to be alarmist . . .'

'Let's hurry, Padre.'

Henry found his son wheeling his bicycle from an outhouse in the grounds of Karachi House. 'Jim, perhaps I haven't any right to ask you for promises. But — would you give me a promise always to look after your mother?'

Almost by habit the old resentment popped out. 'I'm looking after her now.'

'Yes.'

Jim watched the hope die in his father's face. 'Dad —'

''Tis the old cooker, sir.' That moving mountain, Bridie, had appeared from no where. ''Tis no good. Sure, I'll never be after getting the supper ready!'

'Dad, don't worry! I want to have a word with you —'

But Henry was already bustling away towards the kitchen. Here was a coolie needing guidance, and guided he, or rather she, must be.

Jim wheeled his bicycle irresolutely down the drive. The gulls and the gale screamed at one another. At the gate he paused. He recalled a remark he had once made to Jenny: Dad's is a closed mind, a little iron circle of beliefs. Under stress they could even destroy him, because he has no — *give.*

He wheeled his bicycle back again and entered the house. His father had already left the kitchen.

'Hello, darling! Did you come back for something?' His mother sat at her writing-desk in the drawing-room, turning over the pages of a prayer-book.

'Where's Dad?' He quipped uneasily, 'I've sought him high and, though I'm bitterly ashamed to have to confess this, low.'

She looked startled. 'He's just gone out to the car. He's going to take in the boat. Didn't he ask you to help?'

The sound of an engine arose, passing down the drive. 'He obviously assumes I'm on the way to my studio.'

'Oh do hurry, Jim!'

Down at the quay, the boat was plunging at her moorings. A gull swerved through the spray shrieking defiance. There was no sight of his father or the car; perhaps he had stopped off to see the Canon. Dad would call round at the studio for help. He always did. At least he need feel no worry about that. The situation must not be allowed to build up further and get out of hand. What troubles human beings made for themselves, with their large brains and involved sensibilities! What melodramatic creatures they were! To an animal, had it the power of reflection in some limited degree, all this would seem like a storm in a teacup! He would no longer allow resentment to stifle words of cheer and of affection.

He climbed the stairs. Passing his table, he picked up the sheets of notes that Henry had slipped to him in church. He stood at the side window, once again re-reading them. There was a memo as to where he might find documents relating to the past running of the firm; more ominously, there were notes on forward planning.

He looked out of the window. The rain was sluicing clean the soot-corroded slates of the roof tops. Against the dark green background of frantic trees, four strings of bright grey beads held his eye as they moved ceaselessly from left to right. They were raindrops, running down the four telegraph wires of the descending street. The clouds thickened and the wires became invisible, so that the drops seemed to be dim fireflies floating past the boughs.

The gathering dusk roused him. He glanced at his watch; half past five. Still no sign of his father! Instead of closing the shutters, he drew the cotton curtains that his mother had made him. His father would see the light through them. He crossed to draw also the curtains of the window overlooking the harbour. The three-masted schooner lay at anchor upon a sea agitated by the gale to cold stormy silver and pale green. The riding-light suspended from her shrouds was a warm spark in the twilight. A sweep of foam floated, a white splash, upon the violent chop.

Earlier, back in the kitchen at Karachi House, Henry had raised his head from his task. He had switched on the cooker. 'There you are,

102

Bridie! If the mistress asks for me, I've gone down to attend to the boat.' At the door he had paused. 'By the way, did you ever hear what happened about that young fellow who was — who had the accident?'

'Lor' yes, sir, I'm after telling the mistress. Didn't ye hear? Attention was first drawn to his body floating in, be the gulls swooping and screeching and tearing at it. The head was nearly eaten off him be the fish.' She added with relish, 'He nearly floated to his own door.'

Henry, already half out of the kitchen, held his face averted. 'All right, Bridie! I mean to say . . .'

She was not to be denied. ''Tis a grand funeral there was. The relations and neighbours were drinking in the pub till midnight. 'Twas a cousin leapt into the tide, like a fellah that was boozed.' She put back her head and her bosom shook like a mountain in mirth. 'His clothes dragged him under and, sure, he nearly followed his relation.'

Henry, gradually closing the door behind him and presenting only a grim profile, nodded briefly. The woman was all piss and wind!

As he took his yellow oilskins off the peg, he heard Vera clear her throat. He put his hand for a moment on the handle of the drawing-room door, then withdrew it. Pulling on his dark blue peaked seaman's cap, he went out to the garage. Five minutes later the limousine was purring down the hill.

And ten minutes after that, the grey Morris-Cowley jolted to a halt at the gate.

'You wait here, Jenny. I'll walk up and spy out the land.'

'Hello, Padre!' Vera stood at the front door. 'Henry and Jim have just gone down to take in the boat. Come and join me in a cup of tea. Henry'll be back.'

'A bit urgent that I find him. Take you up on that cup of tea another time. See you!'

As he hurried away, he was aware of Vera's worried look following him. But to have lingered and given her the chance to question him would have been worse.

He rejoined Jenny.

*   *   *

Jim's brush moved steadily from palette to canvas. Between each touch he took a step backwards to survey the result. A bowl of oranges and apples, illuminated by a table-lamp of blue and white china with a raffia shade, had been arranged in front of him. The cotton curtains, with their design of blue and yellow flowers, seemed, for all their flimsiness, to provide a barrier against the gale gnawing at the stone corner of the building and the eaves of the roof. So forcibly was the rain being hurled against the window that the water was bubbling up under the bottom edge, running across the sill, and making a darker patch on the pale brown of the floor planking. Light shone through the ventilation holes at the top of his old paraffin stove, giving out yellow heat.

Despite his worry, the memory of the contrast between the warm spark of the schooner's riding-light and the cold of the sea haunted him. Such beauty came seldom, and then unbidden. Shouldn't he now be capturing it on canvas? A still-life could be arranged at any time. He peered out. Gulls, short of fish, shrieked abuse at a lone fisherman on the quay. Four trawlers, the rattle of whose chains he had heard as they dropped anchor, lay parallel to one another. They were ablaze with electric light, which cast a brief gleam on the violent sea streaming past their hulls. It seemed impossible that the single anchor and slender chain of each could hold its great charge of steel and light off the lea shore so close by, towards which their sterns seemed to strain dangerously. Immediately below him, the street lamp lit the slip with the rusty mine case. Surge after surge came out of the darkness and drove up the slip, washing and rewashing its stones to a cleanliness beyond all human scouring.

A tall burly figure in yellow oilskins and a navy blue seafaring cap stood at the top of the quay steps, opposite where the boat was moored. He bent down. His arms began to work to and fro as he hauled on the running-moorings. The dark shape of the boat was moving slowly towards the quay. Held against the lunges of the on-shore wind by the painter rope at its bow, it came in stern first. When the stern was plunging about only a foot from the steps, the man ceased hauling on the moorings, and had straightened up. The street light caught his face. It was indeed his father! Taking in the boat because of bad weather? That was all his eye and Betty Martin! Since when would he be able single-handed, after drifting the

104

sixteen-foot boat down to the slip, to disembark in the wild surge and haul her up? Indeed, since when did his father ever do anything single-handed, if there existed the possibility of rounding up a gang of coolies?

Vera hurried down the hill. The rain made straggles of the luxuriant brown hair at her temples. A scarf was drawn over her head.

Earlier, she had sat at her writing-desk fingering the prayer-book. He had given it to her almost — almost as a keepsake! Come to think of it, he had never committed himself to securing Jim's help; usually, accompanied by much lip twitching, the matter would have been left in no dount. Henry was simply not behaving like a man disappointed in his son, nor even like one worried solely that his son should be exposed to gossip. He was behaving like a man gnawed at by remorse. If his behaviour didn't fit, then neither did Jim's. He wasn't behaving at all like a fellow suffering from remorse. There was the icy calm with which he had made his confession to her; a certain mechanicalness in its recital. There was his, 'Yes, I'm the father,' said without any conviction. He was suffering from a sense of grievance! And what had those whispered exchanges and passing of papers in the church been about?

The lights of Lower Glenmorris came into view. The lines on her forehead deepened and her lips puckered. Despite her nervousness at such times, she herself would help Henry to get in the boat if she couldn't find Jim. As she emerged on to the quay, she saw that there were already floating streaks of seaweed torn up by the storm. At the same moment she saw also a tall figure bowed over the mooring ropes and hauling in the boat. She was still too distant to make out his features in the weak light from the widely spaced standards, but she knew his oilskins. And he was alone!

Now Henry had entered the boat and perched himself up on the bow. He began to haul in on one side of the continuous rope, so that it took the other side, to which the painter was attached, out towards the anchor marked by a buoy. The painter drew the boat after it until the craft was safely beyond the draw on the steps. Then he returned to the centre thwart. He didn't look up as he slipped the rowlocks into their holes on the gunwale. He placed the oars within the row-locks at the ready. He moved back to the bow to cast off the painter.

105

She made a megaphone of her hands. 'Henry! Wait! Wait till I get to the slip! I'll help you pull her up.' The on-shore gale stifled the words in her face.

Loosing the painter, he hurried back to the oars before the wind could whip the boat on to the steps. Hurling his great weight against the oar handles, he gradually opened a gap. Hope returned to her as she saw that he was following a diagonal course which was also taking him towards the slip. For some reason the silly boy, quite madly of course, was trying to take in the boat on his own.

She ran towards the slip. The next moment he was past it and always increasing his distance from the high face of the quay. He was only avoiding rowing directly into the eye of the wind; only shedding part of its force by taking it on his port bow. In that way he would eventually pass down the whole length of the quay, yet always be making larger the stretch of water between them. And next? Across the inner harbour until he reached the shelter of its other side? And so along it until he came to the end of the headland which the schooner had earlier rounded? Then, after a fierce struggle with the gale blasting at the point, into the outer harbour . . .

Fear filled her heart and a sob her throat. 'Oh God, help us! Help us all!'

Jim left the window. He ran across the garret to the nail in the wooden partitioning wall and unhooked his mackintosh and sou'-wester. Buttoning up, he returned to the window. His father was already rowing obliquely against the wind, making almost as much leeway as headway. He ran down the stairs, tying the tapes of his sou'wester under his chin. He would run the length of the quay and on to the pier-head. The latter, jutting forward at rightangles, would close part of the gap between the boat and the quay. His father might see and hear him. As he reached the pier-head, the boat swam past him sideways but now well out. The toiler at the oars never looked up from his task.

He returned to the quay. The storm laughed wildly over the town, spitting fury. Nearby floated two fishing-boats painted in the usual black of Glenmorris. The fishermen always left their oars in them. One of the boats was far too large for him to row. The other was a possibility.

He untied the rope from the iron ring set in the roadway; the fishermen in general didn't use running-moorings. Holding the rope he walked along the quay, hauling the stern round as he did so towards a slipway. As he made his way crabwise down the slip to escape sliding on the bright green weed, the stern was plunging about, only a foot from him.

He leapt. Partly missing an open space in the bouncing craft, he fell over the stern thwart. He lay in the bottom, faint from the gash. Had he broken his leg? Dragging himself up to the bow, he paused amidships to set the oars ready between the wooden thole-pins. The bite of the gale cleared his head. He hauled on the anchor rope. The moment the anchor lifted clear of the sea-bed, the wind whipped the boat towards the quay. Leaving the anchor just as it was, he gave the cable a single turn round the bow thwart and tied a temporary bow-knot. He dragged his way to the centre.

He hurled his twelve and a half stone against the handles of the clumsy narrow-bladed oars. The backwards rush towards the shore arrested, he set himself to the long strain against the blast, which blew him back between strokes almost as far as the stroke had taken him. Like his father, he soon began to shed a part of the pressure by shifting the wind on to his port bow. After he had opened a gap between himself and that menacing weed- and limpet-covered wall, he completed the lifting of the anchor. This time he moved more easily; his leg had been only numbed. Here and there he saw a gleam of light from some yacht whose owner was aboard, making his craft fast against the storm.

His oar strokes changed from a long sweep to a short jerk. The heavy boat built up the fatigue in his shoulders and arms into a continuous burning pain. How could he ever overtake his father, equipped not only with magnificent strength and superior weight, but also with spoon-bladed oars and a light clinker-built boat?

Abruptly he ceased rowing. The spray-broken chop, streaming back continuously in the direction of the quay, rapidly took back all that he had wrung out of the blast. In wild grief he looked this way and that. He thought of his father's frustrated attempts to make amends. He thought of his mother, doubtless seated at this moment alone in her drawing-room. He would be responsible for the more terrible loneliness that was about to descend on her.

He began to use the long narrow oar blades to guide his sternwards drift towards a glow emanating from one of the yachts. Would the owner face the weather? How could he ask him to, without revealing that strange matters were afoot?

Two figures in oilskins moved about the cockpit. The groan of the oars between the thole-pins as he manoeuvred, made them turn their faces. He grabbed one of the shrouds and spilled out his fears.

'Right, Jim!' The padre's voice was steady, cheerful. 'We'll get after him. Make your boat fast to my moorings.'

When Vera had told Canon Moss that Henry and Jim were taking in their boat, two thoughts had occurred to the padre. The first was that Henry would do nothing drastic while his son was with him. The second was that he too should secure the safety of his own craft, particularly as Jenny his 'crew' happened to be there to help him.

'Jenny, I'll use the punt to put you ashore. You could shelter in the florists'. Seem to be still open. Light in their window.'

'No, Padre!' Her agitated fingers pressed the damp out of the golden fringe that emerged from under her black sou'wester. 'We must get away at once.'

Eyebrows bushed down over small grey eyes. 'I'm a soldier. Women must be got to the rear first. Then the men can get on with the job.' There followed the high thin laugh.

But violet eyes gazed back steadily. Another representative of the tribe of men, albeit a nice one, trying to manage her! 'I'm going along. I'm responsible to Vera.' *Had* the padre guessed? If so, her remark would confirm his guess.

'I'm responsible to your mother.' This time there was no laugh.

'I'm going along, Padre.'

He regarded her. Abruptly he produced his pipe and inserted it into the convenient gap in his teeth. 'Let's get the cover off the mainsail, Jim.'

As Henry had earlier hauled in the moorings of his boat, he had said to himself: they told me that I'd drown if I tried to row round Masterman buoy in an open canoe and a stiff chop. But I did it. Now I shall row round Masterman and back in a boat, only in the middle of a storm. He had once told the padre he would do it. If anything — happened — to him, no one would say that he . . . It would, if it happened, be a pure accident. There was no sin in having a sense of adventure. Vera would be paid on his life insurance, and on the additional annuity he had purchased. Jim would keep the business going.

He could see again in his mind's eye the red wooden lattice-work that formed the top of the buoy. On a strip of timber nailed to the lattice-work was the single word, MASTERMAN. In the centre of this superstructure was the round metal siren which sucked in air as the buoy rose on each roller, and let it out in a warning moan to shipping as it sank down again. The great metal base, trailing locks of seaweed, heaved ponderously out of the sucking wavelets, then settled down into them once more.

Taking the oars, he bent to the task. His ears were filled with the distant moan of Masterman. Great seas of sound rolled in from the harbour mouth. Shedding the load by half running with the wind where he must, making use of the shelter of the land where he could, he reached the end of the headland that divided off the inner harbour from the outer. He rested in the quiet water under its lea. Then, keeping only two-oars' length from the shore to escape the draw on the rocks yet reduce the arc to a minimum, he hurled himself into the task of taking the boat right into the eye of the wind and wrenching her round the headland. This he seemed to have succeeded in doing. But an eccentric air current, coming over some low-lying land, drove him out. As he endeavoured to push on and at the same time to regain his inshore position, his motion became only more and more a sideways drift into the centre of the harbour across the dim expanse of white crests.

He rested on his oars to allow the ache to die from his arms. He undid a few buttons of his oilskins and, through force of habit, brought out his gold fob watch. Then the strange thought came to him that time no longer mattered. Time not matter! What would his father, who had left him the watch, have said? He put it away unglanced at and resumed rowing.

More and more he forgot about Masterman as his thoughts turned inwards to the picture in his mind. It was of something that floated just at the surface, so that ripples occasionally lapped over it. Gulls screamed and wheeled about it. He looked closer. He saw the half-naked body blown out with putrefaction and, after crabs had crawled over it in their silent feast, all that was left of a man's face. To float back thus to the eyes of his wife and his son, to the town that knew the repute of his family and the triumph of his career . . .

He heard himself scream as the blade of his oar struck against something that floated just at the surface of the water. Throwing all his strength against his port oar, he veered away in a terror of revulsion. His blade again struck the object. The moon had come up behind the storm rack and was charging across the sky, its disk scything through vapour. By its light he could see that it was a punt that had swamped at her moorings and was floating filled to the gunwales. He must have drifted right across the harbour to the opposite shore. His mind turned away from it to the contemplation of its own nightmare. Could it have been *he* who had screamed? In all his grown-up life such a sound had never issued from his lips! But his mind was in too high fever to dwell on anything long.

He glanced over his shoulder. The knife-edge of the bastion of King William Fort rose up sheer, its top a threat against the luminous sky. It would be a cleaner way . . . He fought on into the foam-crested night towards the foot of the bastion. The harsh faces of rocks, bearded with seaweed, grimly faced the battering of masses of water that writhed back like serpents, poised, then struck again and again.

He was in the act of bracing the oar-handle (the delicate spoon-bladed end must not be used) against a rock, to resist the too-violent sweeping in of the boat, when his mind cleared as some pulse of vigour emerged from that magnificent reserve. God was not destroying him! He was destroying himself. Hadn't he said to Jenny, 'It would have been a sin'? It was God's will that a man should endure, and serve. He was a poor thing; always had been. All piss and wind.

He pushed off. But at that moment a wave was rushing in. He leapt out on to some submerged rocks, the water tugging at his legs. He gripped the gunwale with both hands, fending off the boat. The withdrawing wave sucked her irresistibly out again, and he was dragged with her. For a moment he was insulated from the winter sea by his clothes. Then it began to introduce tiny icy searching tentacles through the cloth, tentacles that grew by strides into fingers, and then into hands, and then into arms, that clung to him and squeezed out the warmth of his body. A plank must have been staved in, for the boat was settling. She was drifting towards the inner harbour. His fingers were rigid claws. If they slipped from the gunwale, odium would be heaped upon his son. It would be said that his son's conduct with Jenny had driven his father . . . Even Vera would think it. Unless the boy told . . . But the boy would never tell, nor allow Jenny to tell.

He reminded himself of the fuss that people had made about his periodic swims off the pier-head after office hours, when he had extended them into the winter. One of the protesters had announced, with a grave shake of his head, that a friend of his who had tried it had developed pneuomonia by November. A second had announced, with a gloomy look, that a cousin was dead by December. Henry's stiffening facial muscles managed a smile. He'd show them! He was indestructible.

His thoughts became less coherent, and also very simple. Everything else left his mind, and he thought only of his wife and his son. It would be so much easier to yield to the drowsiness. But he must hold on till nearer the quay. Then it might be said that it was an accident while getting into the boat.

His white fingers slipped from the gunwale. The boat floated away. The bitter water flowed in between his parted lips . . .

By good fortune there had been one reef in the mainsail. They had not dared to spend time on taking in the second. The padre threw one leg over the tiller to hold it in position, while he took both hands to hauling in the mainsail. The rope forming the main-sheet squeaked over the pulleys. The boom, the great spar at the foot of the sail, moved in slowly. The sail itself was a tall silhouette against the rack flying across the face of a fitful moon. The padre put down his leg and seemed to collapse a little over the tiller.

From running on an even keel, the craft now heeled over until it appeared that she must capsize. Jim, crouched to leeward as he drew taut the foresheet and made it fast, glanced at the dark water glinting but a foot or two from him. It boiled up over the side and right on to the half-decking, prevented from washing into the cockpit only by the four-inch-high strip of coaming running round it. He winced as the cold water slapped him in the face; she had taken a sea over

111

her bows. He turned sternwards. The angle of heel was so steep, that the padre and Jenny were all but in a standing attitude as they half sat on the seat running along the port side, with their legs stretched across the breadth of the cockpit and their feet braced against the edge of the seat running along the starboard. He scrambled his way to them, clinging to the coaming, the rubber soles of his shoes slipping on the spray-dampened ceiling-boards.

The padre's grey eyes, almost buried in the contracted bushy eyebrows, cocked themselves on the sail. 'Ought to take in a reef, Jim. Don't like to do it in this sea.'

They left the spark of the schooner and the blaze of the trawlers behind them. A greater darkness on the dark surface of the water travelled across. A sharp creak from the far from sound rigging (the padre had been no better endowed in the matter of yachts than cars), as the squall struck the boat, caused Jim to raise his head. The silhouettes of the mast top and the peak of the sail described a downwards arc across the sky. His fingers whitened upon the coaming as the yacht lay flat over. His mouth opened as the sea rose up before him. He was about to be precipitated forward on to his face into the foaming water. He didn't notice Jenny cling to his arm.

The padre lunged forward, pushing the tiller over. The old yacht, answering her helm sluggishly, moved round into the eye of the wind, spilling the pressure out of her sails. She recovered on to an even keel. The whole air above Jim's head seemed to be filled with the shuddering of the thick dimly seen canvas, darkened with spray to half its height, like that of something uncontrollable and alive.

He turned to the padre for instructions. Canon Moss's face seemed to be shining with moisture. For a moment Jim took it for spray. Then he realised that it was sweat.

'What is it, Padre?'

'M' chest, Jim.' He gasped. 'M' heart's giving me gyp.'

'I'll take over, Padre.'

'No, no, Jim, you couldn't. Haven't had the experience.' Canon Moss attempted cheerfulness. He searched his uncertain memory. 'As what's-his-name wrote, "And all I want is a something ship, And a rudder to steer her by." I expect you learned that at school, Jenny.'

'Er — yes.' She flicked a half smile at Jim. 'Something like it.'

The boat re-gathered way as Canon Moss let her bow pay off.

But five minutes later the tiller was put down again and the mainsail close-hauled as another shadow flew over the sea.

'We're not making much progress.' Jim's features were peaked with anxiety.

'We'll have to shorten sail.'

Jim gazed at the great expanse of canvas, hauled in flat and hard as a board. Getting a grip with numb fingers on that wet surface! Controlling its furious undulations when the yacht would be turned into the eye of the wind! But together Jim and Jenny subdued the canvas, a powerful beast attempting to evade capture, into the confines of the second reef.

Although, now that the sail had been made smaller, moving more easily, the craft still lay over, though not so perilously, before the next squall. One of the ponderous pigs of iron in the centre of the cockpit, provided as extra ballast, broke from its rusted wire fastening. It slid down the sloping floor and struck the side of the hull.

'That'll hole her, Padre.'

'Better leave it where it is, Jim, if it will stay. You could never shift it.' A moment later he sang out, 'Stand by!'

Jenny bowed her head and gripped the coaming. Jim made his way forward.

'About she goes,' cried the padre.

Jenny and he scrambled to the opposite seat as the yacht heeled over towards the side on which they had just been sitting. They were away on the new tack.

Jim looked round at a cry from Jenny. The pig of iron was slithering across under the compulsion of the new direction of slope. It struck the hull planking heavily.

The padre's face was grave. 'Can you secure it, Jim? 'Fraid I shouldn't be much use. Chest's grown very painful.'

The weight secured, there ensued the struggle into the gale. The padre drove and coaxed that old tub with no less fortitude than he drove and coaxed his ancient Morris Cowley. Amidst the wretchedness of anxiety and the worsening weather, Jim took comfort from the sight of the great hairy skilful hand upon the tiller; the empty pipe, bowl upside down to keep it dry, clenched in the strong jaw; the tough features presented steadfastly to the elements, rivulets of moisture running down them like water down a rock.

'Ought to make your father on this tack,' cried the padre cheerfully; and, when they did not, equally cheerfully, 'Well, we'll certainly make him on the next.' His own pain put aside, his ugly features lit with a radiance that no dusk could cover, his cheery voice, crying 'Stand by! About she goes!', filled with a gospel of hope, he sat, hand firm on the tiller like some saint of old, guiding them through wind and wave.

'Padre, there's something ahead!'

'Take the torch, Jim.'

In the circle of light, Henry's face was ashen. His eyes closed, he rested his chin on the gunwale of the boat that his oar had touched; the punt that had swamped at her moorings. His clutching fingers were rigid claws. At the stimulation of the light, he opened his eyes. They seemed to Jim to be filled with an urgent message.

'Hold on, Dad! Hold on!' A sob burst from him.

His right foot on the seat, his left out on the half-decking, he caught his father with both hands under the left armpit. He eased him away from the punt, turning him as he did so, and brought him chest first alongside the yacht. The sodden coldness of his clothing filled him with despair. How much life could still remain? One hand now under each armpit, he partly drew him on to the narrow strip of the half-decking. The more he got his father clear of the water, the more he lost the assistance of its support. He could move him no further.

Suddenly a pair of gloved hands appeared beside his; small hands that gripped under his father's arm, leaving him free to improve his position and lift powerfully with both hands under the other. Henry's great inert form was bundled, albeit as gently as possible, into the bottom of the cockpit.

'Lay him face downwards. Turn his head sideways.' The padre swept the yacht round. 'Press down on, and then release, his back just behind his lungs. Keep time with normal deep breathing. Squeeze out any water. That's it!' They were tearing along for home before the gale, great following seas running up under their counter and lifting them on. 'Turn him over on his back. No! Better leave him like that; we don't want him to swallow his tongue. Cover him with the tarpaulin. In the bow locker.'

114

Again Jim found the gloved hands beside him, hauling out the heavy material from the space under the bow decking. 'Thanks, Jenny.' He kept his voice low. 'You were wonderful. In your — things being the way with you as they are, you might have injured yourself.'

'Hardly likely.'

'What's that?'

'No baby, it seems.'

'No baby!' He stared at the bitterness in her face. 'What about the sickness in the office? What about —'

'A false pregnancy. I've been to see Dr O'Grady.'

'I can't believe it! Is Dr O'Grady sure —'

'I've had one before. Dr O'Grady knew. Mummy and Canon Moss knew.'

'You've had one before! How could you have had one before? You haven't surely before been with . . .'

'We used to have a bitch. She nearly died having her last litter. So we didn't dare to let her breed again. But although she hadn't "been with", as you put it, she had several phantom pregnancies. Nature takes over.'

'You surely claim to have more sense than a dog!'

'I wonder. The symptoms arise willy-nilly, especially when I wanted them so much. I was much younger then. And even more foolish.'

'You didn't check up this time? You didn't let Dad know? He may die!'

'The padre's been trying all the afternoon to contact him.'

'Good God, Dad's been at home half the afternoon!'

'And out in bursts the other half. The padre couldn't say anything to your mother. Nor could he trace your father in the town.'

'Why didn't you check up weeks ago?'

She lowered her head. The peak of the black sou'wester hid her face. 'I felt so certain I was pregnant. This time there was cause. If only Mummy had called in Dr O'Grady again! She made a show of questioning me, but deep down she was pleased.'

'Take over at the fore-sheets. I'd like to be alone with my father.'

'Jim, I'm sorry —'

'Please! Leave me alone with my father.' His voice trembled.

She moved up close to the fore-deck.

There was a bruise over one of Henry's eyebrows, and a cut across his cheek, but his face was too cold to bleed. His father, his dear imperfect father, storm-racked, his progenitor, the hitherto sturdy bearer of the family's fortunes! Some day he must say goodbye to him, perhaps that very day. Then, the shelter and the leader removed, he himself would be the elder generation.

'Stand by with the boat-hook, Jim!' It was the Canon.

He looked up to see that they were sweeping down on their moorings under the compulsion of a sudden tremendous squall. The waves, white claws unsheathed, humped their green backs, the spume rising off them like bristling hair, then sprang with a roar at the slips and quay. They snarled over the top, savaging the broken roadway. The gale too growled in the gutters and grabbed at the roofs. Everywhere the fangs of the storm gleamed, like a tiger kill in the moonlight.

He extracted the boat-hook from the forward locker and clambered on to the bow decking.

Canon Moss mopped with his handkerchief at the creases and folds of his face and at his bull neck. Rounding the moorings, he brought the little yacht up into the wind, where she momentarily floated motionless, her canvas undulating violently. Jim hooked up the mooring rope, shared by the fishing-boat and the padre's punt. He brought it in over the bow and made it fast. Canon Moss and Jenny, moving gingerly round Henry's form, lowered the mainsail.

The squall had passed over. But how to get ashore and into warmth, through the abated but still violent rush and retreat of the sea on the slipway, the unconscious and massive Henry, now dying of cold?

116

Chapter Nine

The first idea that flitted into the twilight of Henry's mind, intensifying then fading, but finally forming, was of a block of ice encircled by a ring of fire. Despite the licking of the flames, the ice remained firm and white. Gradually he came to the conclusion that both were in a laundry.

He began to identify himself with the ice. That was it! He was cold. He was cold to the very innermost parts of his body; cold as he had never been before. But there was heat. He was ringed with heat. The heat seemed to be battering at the numb periphery of his body, seeking to storm an entry into the fortress of cold. Presently it produced enough feeling for him to realise that there was a great weight upon him. And always there was the laundry smell.

He perceived that the surrounding heat was not a ring about him. Rather, though it was assaulting the walls of his body from all directions, it was pressing its attack with especial vigour at a number of points. Two of these points were the palms of his hands. He exerted himself and his fingers moved a little. Their pads were too numb to identify textures, but the mound under each palm gave before the slight pressure. There was a mound of heat against the sole of each of his feet. He explored with his toes. These mounds were flexible also. Two more of them were tucked into the small of his back, one on each side. The back of each of his thighs rested on a mound.

Through his closed eyelids he became aware of light. It was an intense light. Probably it was sunlight streaming in through the window of the laundry. Would he be able to open his eyes? His face was rigid, his teeth clenched. His muscles began to shudder. After a struggle his lids unglued sufficiently to establish that he couldn't bear the intense white light and must hastily close them again.

He turned his head away from the sunshine. He opened his eyes a little wider this time. He saw a table with apples and oranges arranged in a bowl and, standing by them, an unlit table-lamp with a blue and white china base and a raffia shade. There were also tubes of paint and brushes in jam jars, all of which struck him as odd in a laundry. His eyes were adjusted enough now to challenge the light. He saw that the 'sun' was an unshaded electric bulb, tinted blue to simulate sunshine, hanging from the centre of the ceiling.

His gaze travelled round the room. It dwelt for a moment on the pipe gripped in the padre's teeth, then on the fag hanging from the corner of Mildred's mouth, and finally came to rest on Jim's cheroot. He attempted to warn these people against the dangers of their habit. But, though his teeth had unsealed, they were chattering so violently that he couldn't talk. Why was the boy grinning?

He heard him speak. 'Dad's going to be all right, Jenny. But we must get some more warmth into him. I think a cup of tea is indicated.'

Jenny! Henry turned his eyes once more to the table. How did she get here? A parcel lay beside her. Or, rather, a paper wrapping which appeared to enclose flowers. How did *all* these people get here? Her hair gleamed pale gold in the stark light. Her dark eyes rested on him anxiously. Her soft hand, that hand that had, in the partial absence of his wife, so consoled him when he held it, lifted a kettle from the top of a small paraffin stove that stood on the table. The yellow heat warmed the pallor of her face. There was a teapot near the bowl of apples and oranges and the table-lamp. What were paint-brushes and a bowl of fruit doing in a laundry? Reminded him, rather, of Jim's studio.

The boy was stubbing out his cheroot. He was limping over to him with a cup of tea. Why was he limping? When had he hurt himself?

'Now, Dad, hot tea with lots of sugar!'

Henry tried to give his double nod, but his head hardly seemed to move. He watched his son put the cup and saucer down in the planks of the floor.

The boy was wrinkling up his nose. 'Smells like a laundry here! I didn't try to take off your wet underwear; it was clinging to you.

I just piled on top of you everything I could lay my hands on: blankets, rugs, overcoats, mackintoshes, jackets.'

Henry felt a strong arm encircle his shoulders, raising him to a sitting position. Pillows and cushions were thrust into the small of his back, so that two of the mounts pressed against him even more closely. Whatever he was lying on swayed and creaked a little under his weight. It swayed and creaked again as his son engineered himself on to its edge, and Henry caught a glimpse of canvas stretched over wood. It was the boy's camp-bed, on which he slept at his studio! With his other hand Jim picked up the cup off its saucer.

'I'd better test this first for heat.' Smiling, he swivelled the cup so that he sipped from a different part of the rim. 'Seems all right.'

The forceful Henry found it not altogether agreeable being nursed like a child, the tea coaxed between his chattering teeth. But that liquid heat penetrating into the very heart of the fortress was wonderful.

Suddenly a voice trumpeted, 'Ought to see Dr O'Grady, Hampton.'

'Not going to see any doctor, Padre,' Henry growled into his cup. As the chattering abated, his voice was beginning to return, but he knew that it was still too weak to be heard.

His resentment passed as he noted that Canon Moss was slumped rather than seated in Jim's wickerwork chair. Had he had another heart attack? And why, precisely, did he want him to see a doctor?

At all events Canon Moss was vigorous enough to thrust out his jaw. 'You may be well padded, like m'self! I know you do those winter bathes of yours off the pier-head, but . . .'

'I'm not seeing Dr O'Grady.' This time his voice came stronger. 'If I've a sore toe, he examines my head.'

'Shouldn't wonder if he isn't right!' The shot-out tongue was snapped back.

Canon Moss's high thin laugh mingled with Mildred's giggle.

Henry looked at her sharply. The movement of her lips had dislodged the growing length of ash at the end of her cigarette. The ash showered down on one of those revolting little dogs of hers that was lying on her lap. Why wasn't she at home, looking after his property for a change! 'How did you get down?'

Quickly, the padre intervened. 'Told her you'd had a bit of a ducking. Also, Jim wanted hot-water bottles. Hadn't enough at the rectory. Had to explain anyway why Jenny'd be home late. Some fishermen came along and helped us to get you out of the yacht and up the stairs.'

Henry had a vision of the Morris Cowley back-firing its way up the hill (its magneto for ever needed re-timing), then returning cargoed with hot-water bottles and a Mildred insisting, as usual, in poking her nose into everything.

Had a bit of a ducking! Henry's brown eyes swept over his son, Jenny, the padre. Of course! He's fallen into the water. Somehow they must have saved him. At some risk to thir lives too. The wind was still clawing at the eaves. Gusts, filled with rain, hurled themselves at the window panes. If these fine people had risked their lives to save him, there must be some use to his living.

His gaze inadvertently turned on Mildred. The blasted woman had caught his glance. That, of course, would start things up! Always terrified that he was going to whip away her house from her! Serve her right if he did! But of course he'd never dream of doing so, if only for Jenny's sake. Yes, here it came! Mildred was jingling her bangles; that meant that she was about to exercise her feminine charm. She was turning her face away from the cold light of the blue-tinted bulb towards the warmer light from the stove. Her alleged milkmaid complexion was about to be exhibited. She was tossing scent from her hair in his direction. All this was not unusual. But why such a concentrated display at this particular moment?

Who could guess? Certainly not Henry, who of course didn't yet know that there was to be no baby. But — Mildred did . . . So was she thinking that now that there was to be no baby, perhaps also there would be no marriage? Still worse, when Jim and his parents found out that they had suffered such an upset for nothing, might they not actually turn against Jenny? They might even turn against Mildred herself, saying that it was her duty as Jenny's mother to have had the doctor in earlier.

She was now, Henry observed, beginning to frisk about the studio. It could mean only that she was threatening to display her racehorse ankles. She started to whinny over the pictures. So that was it! Jim also must be wooed, to consolidate the marriage with Jenny. 'Ah, for goodness sake, woman . . .' It was a grumble in his throat.

Mildred was throwing girlish glances at his son. 'I wish I had your talent! I don't fully understand modern painting.'

'Yankee pictures!' The padre's laugh mingled with the sound of the door's opening.

Henry felt a quiver in his son's long fingers. They abruptly ceased wiping with a handkerchief the tea from his moustache and beard. He followed his gaze. Vera stood on the threshold.

Her slender figure was evening-gowned under her overcoat; she had done her usual change for evening dinner after he had left Karachi House. The rain had made straggles of the thick brown hair emerging at her temples from under her head scarf.

Seeing her husband's eyes on the bedraggled hem of her gown, she said, 'I was trying to get someone to put me aboard the motor-boat. I was going to come after you if it wasn't locked up.'

Henry felt the camp-bed heave upwards as Jim rose off its edge, leaving the cup in his father's now firmer grasp. The boy was watching his parents, his fingers tweaking at his bow-tie.

Canon Moss, his great expanse of chest and stomach clothed in a fisherman's sweater, had groaned his way to his feet amidst a formidable creaking of wickerwork. 'We called round for you at Karachi House. Bridie said you'd gone down to the quay. Gave us four hot-water bottles for this man.' He pointed at Henry with the stem of his pipe. 'Jim insisted on a hot-water bottle at each of what he called the heat spots. When we got down again to the quay we couldn't see you.'

She smiled fleetingly. 'Sit down, Padre. You look all in.'

He subsided gratefully.

Henry watched his wife. He saw her turn away. She had been up to the church. But the pew she had prayed in was not the pew in which she had kneeled beside Henry for a quarter of a century. It had been one on the other side of the aisle. There she had knelt as a girl with her parents and her brothers. Her prayer had been not only for Henry and his rescuers. She had prayed for herself too. As she left the church, she was weeping.

'I got a message that you four had come in.' Her first wild feeling of relief was abating.

Four! Henry's eyes swept over his son, Jenny, the padre, Mildred.

Mildred wouldn't put out to sea in a flat calm! Who, then, was the fourth? Himself, of course!

He noticed that Jenny had risen from her perch on the edge of the table. She was fiddling with the gold fringe at her brow, as she looked at his wife. 'I drew the curtains to let you see the light.'

Vera stared at her. 'I'd seen the light before.'

As his wife advanced towards him, Henry bent forward and replaced his cup in its saucer on the floor. I'd seen the light before — what did she mean by that? Had she guessed . . . As he straightened up again, he saw that she had paused to put her hands on Jim's shoulders. His jacket was rough amd masculine beneath her palms. She stood on tiptoe and kissed him on the forehead. He was her hope, her future.

Jim was staring at her. Surprised by the warmth of the kiss? Perhaps the boy was wondering what in particular had occasioned its warmth. That he had helped in the rescue of his father? Or that he had been tending him as she entered? Or was it because . . . At all events his son bent forward and, for a moment, put his arms about her.

Canon Moss scratched his head with the stem of his pipe. 'I've told that man that he ought to see the doctor.'

'Oh no, Padre!' Vera's brow furrowed. 'We don't want this getting out more than it need. You know the kind of thing people will say.'

Mildred's eyes were aglow with puzzlement. 'Why should people say anything?'

'I rowed out to look at the schooner and the trawlers.' Henry spoke abruptly. 'I even thought of rowing the boat round Masterman in this storm, just as I once rowed the canoe. Next thing I knew, I was taking an unwanted bath. Tch!'

Jim, now by Jenny at the table, topped up his cooling cup of tea. He glanced at his father. It was all baloney, of course, but splendid baloney, magnificent all his eye and Betty Martin. His father was now nearer to the truth than he had ever been when he was lying to himself.

The padre was studying the bowl of his pipe, his jaw moving in and out like a piston.

'You've been wonderful, Padre; you and Jim.' Vera's cheekbones burned.

Henry watched Jenny uneasily. How would she take her exclusion? She was standing very still.

He noticed that his son was watching too. 'The padre was indeed wonderful. So was Jenny. Without her help, I could never have got Dad on board.' Whatever his differences with her, justice must be done.

Vera turned. 'I hope you make Jim a good wife, Jenny. He's the finest boy in the world.'

With pain, Jenny observed her rearranging under her chin the knot of her scarf, so that the movement of her hands might conceal her trembling lips. I'd seen the light before — was she thinking that Jenny's womb held the child that she had not been able to have herself? Perhaps thinking also: what price now that it was *his* fault that we have had only one? She swung round abruptly and walked away a few paces.

The padre, his eyes rolling up until the whites below showed, stared unseeingly at the ceiling.

Henry could hardly recognise his gentle dignified wife; she had been almost vicious! He glanced at Jenny. Her strong young hands were gripping the edge of the table. The flowers beside her looked like — roses! Though remaining silent with flushed cheeks, nevertheless she had met Vera's onslaught with resolute eyes. Doubtless she felt that Vera had a right to her bitterness.

His wife, as she turned to face the company once more, bit her lip. She would be thinking that forgiveness was demanded of her by her religion. Perhaps even that it was demanded of her by the fact that she had been unable to give him a full married life. By the fact that Jenny was about to become Jim's wife. By the example of the boy's devotion.

She seemed to recover her composure. 'You'll both have to live in Dublin for a spell. Get out of the gossip.'

The golden fringe was shaken decisively. 'No,' said Jenny. 'I'm going to stay right here in Glenmorris every hour of every day, and every hour of every night. I'm going to turn up to work daily, from morning till evening, keeping myself right under the hot little eyeballs of the gossips. They'll wait and wait for a marriage to Jim, and there'll be no marriage —'

'What!' There was a sharp creak from the camp-bed as Henry pushed aside the mountain of bedding.

He saw his son put out his hand quickly and touch her. 'There's no need for that, Jenny!'

Again the resolute shake of the fringe. 'No, Jim, no marriage. And the gossips will wait and wait for a baby, and there'll be no baby —'

'What's this?' Henry manoeuvred his legs over the side of the bed so that he sat upright on its edge, his fourteen stone causing it to sag alarmingly. He saw that his wife was staring, dumbfounded, at the young girl.

The fringe was continuing. '— so they'll try to think of a time when there might have been an abortion, or a birth, or an adoption, and there will be no such time.'

'Wouldn't it,' ventured Mildred, her hopes falling in ruins about her, 'be enough to deny the rumours?'

'No,' burst in Jim. 'That would be to recognise the right of gossips to set themselves up as judges over their neighbours. They are due for no answers and for no explanations.'

The padre gave his high thin laugh. 'Judge not, that ye be not judged.'

'What *is* all this?' Henry's lip twitched. 'I mean to say . . .'

Canon Moss rearranged himself in his chair. 'Jenny's just been to see Dr O'Grady. Phantom pregnancy. Had one before. I called round twice to see you. Even tried down in the town.'

'No baby,' cried Vera. 'All this for no baby! It would be funny if it wasn't so miserable.'

Mildred rushed to intervene. 'I asked Jenny if she was sure. I asked her if she didn't think that it might be the previous time all over again.'

Jenny stared at her. 'Are you trying to sell me down the river, Mummy? At the time, you were hardly able to wait to accept my word. You never lifted so much as a finger to make me check.'

'That's no way to speak to me.'

'To tell the truth is generally a very good way to speak to anyone.'

The padre, his lips shooting in and out, wickerworked his way to his feet. 'Time we got that man home.'

Henry rose amidst the creaking of canvas and wood. Out of the mound that had been piled on top of him he selected a grey ex- army blanket. He pulled it about his shoulders.

'Henry, are you up to it yet?'

He glanced at Vera uneasily. 'Ah, woman! I mean to say . . .' He grumbled his way unconvincingly towards the door.

Reclaiming her hot-water bottles, she followed.

The padre, elaborately shading his eyes from Jim's spectacular waistcoat, relieved him of Henry's sodden outer clothing. 'I'll take these. You see Jenny down.'

Henry felt his wife, descending the staircase behind him, engineer the jacket of his oilskins on to his shoulders over the blanket. The padre's heavy plod could be heard, but some distance away. He was doubtless discreetly leaving them together.

'Got a slow puncture in m' tyre,' he called back cheerfully to those still in the studio, 'but I think it should hold. Come along, Mildred. I'll see you down.'

Mildred clop-clopped indignantly out of the studio. Hadn't lifted a finger to make her check, indeed! Jenny biting the hand that had fed and raised her! If Mildred lost her home, it would be her own daughter who had caused it to happen!

Henry glanced at his wife. Her tall heels tapped on the uncarpeted stairs. At the bottom he paused. 'Look here, Vera, it's only right that you should know —'

'Haven't you done enough, without crossing t's and dotting i's?'

He started at the sharpness of her tone. 'I owed it to you —'

'To me? Or to yourself? Leave me alone. I can't take any more.' She walked rapidly towards where he had left the car before he had entered the boat. 'And what life did you envisage for me if you had died?' The words came from over her shoulder.

So she knew about that too! 'You might have been better off without me,' he muttered.

'Did you imagine my re-marrying — me, with my blinding beauty? Having a string of children — me, with my uncontrollable fertility?'

'You're not to talk about yourself like that!' It was a shout. 'You're a magnificent-looking woman, magnificent. You've had a child. Only one? Who's to say it isn't me? Who says that everything's all right with me?'

He passed her. Trembling, he stood gripping the handle of the car door, his knuckles white. A gust of wind caught the oilskin about his shoulders and set it flapping.

She touched his arm. 'You're a silly boy.'

'I changed my mind. I was trying to get back.'

She went round to the driving seat. 'Fair's fair. I never gave you much of a chance. I wanted to, but somehow I just didn't seem able to manage it. I dare say I need psychoanalysing.'

'Certainly not.'

'Let's go home, old boy. Let's go home.'

Jim followed Jenny down the stairs. He glanced at the roses she carried — red roses. She had slipped out earlier and knocked up the florists, who lived above the shop. He looked at the brushed silk of her hair. Because of the very troubles that had united and divided them, she had been for a long time intensely present in his mind, and a future without her stretched ahead of him like flat winter fields under a grey sky.

'No need to put off getting married, Jenny.'

They had reached a landing.

She turned round. 'After all I've done!'

'It was a nightmare for all of us. Nightmares pass.'

'Jim — Jim, because I'm fairly pretty, I think your father and you tend to read more into me than there is. I'm just not a very noble person. Besides, you don't love me.'

'What's love?'

'You don't know?'

'No. But I'll tell you what I do know. I know that I couldn't even begin to imagine myself marrying anyone else. I know that if ever you left Glenmorris, the whole town would become empty for me.'

'Jim! You'd be up in your attic painting still-lives and seascapes for all you were worth! You'd be cycling to Crosshaven for dances in the Yacht Club, or to Bandon for tennis. You'd be —'

He wasn't listening. 'I'd walk along the harbour road in the evening hoping to meet you, and you wouldn't be there. I'd arrive at the office in the morning, and your desk would be empty. After church I'd look for you on the drive, and see only your mother alone. I'd pass your house, and have to remind myself that you were no longer in it.'

The padre's trumpet ascended the stairway. 'Jim! Jenny! Shake a leg, you two.'

Jim started. He resumed the descent.

He heard Jenny's quick light footstep as she caught up with him. He felt her hand encompass his. 'Jim, that *is* love. But give us time. We both need time.'

'Yes. Jenny . . . Jenny, is it wise to put those flowers on your desk tomorrow?'

'He gave me red roses, and I threw them away. Now they will be back again.'

'Mightn't they stir up painful memories?'

'He gave me red roses, and he nearly died. They go on my desk.'

He looked at the tilt of her chin. 'Okay. Okay.'

Outside, the padre stood with his head thrust inside the bonnet of the Morris Cowley. His voice came to them muffled, but with its eternal sanguine. 'Shall have to clean the plugs. That's what's stopping her.'

He emerged and began scraping with his penknife the top of the plug which he had extracted. He set the gap between the points to the correct fineness by slipping the edge of the blade between them and then pressing in one of them. But when the plugs were clean, it would be the turn of the carburettor to develop a choke, and when that was put right, it would be the magneto that needed re-timing. The words 'plugs', 'carburettor', 'magneto', 'puncture in m' tyre', seemed to have echoed down the years of Jim's and Jenny's childhoods. Perhaps they perceived now that it was symptomatic of the padre's life, the cheerfulness with which he toiled to keep the old wreck on the road, envying no other man his automobile, cursing not his fate that he couldn't afford to have his own serviced by a garage, content with the Morris Cowley to which it had pleased God to call him, a clumsy-fingered, hairy-handed, bulldog-visaged saint, toiling in carbon and grease.

He straightened up. His wild grey eyebrows glistened with droplets from the blown spray. He noted with satisfaction both of Jenny's arms entwined about Jim's arm.

'Jim, your mother drove your father straight up.' He busied his thick fingers in securing down the bonnet with string (the catches had long ceased to work), in order to avoid the appearance of prying into their feelings. 'Hop in, Jenny. I'm taking your mother and you up.'

If the padre didn't pry, Mildred's eyes were filled with a conflict between puzzlement and hope.

Suddenly Canon Moss approached the young people. 'Don't underestimate time.' The lowness of his voice only emphasised its earnestness. 'Time softens all the hard edges. Time lessens painful memories and then cures them. It's God's greatest gift to Man. You'd be most foolish to underestimate the passing of time; the blessed passing of time.'

Jim watched the lop-sided rear of the Morris depart. A street lamp, suspended from the centre of a wire stretched across the roadway, rocked violently, hurling the shadows about. The padre half heaved himself round to wave a hairy paw out of the window. The Morris, after performing a spectacular swerve on the fortunately deserted quay, vanished round a corner.

Jim, making his way along the quay, as though the retreating car were a magnet drawing him on, bowed his sou'westered head against the gale. The Morris Cowley would now be labouring up the hill on too high a gear in the belief that this would save petrol, the Canon swaying to and fro over the wheel to give it a phantom boost.

The tall lean figure turned into the shelter formed by the sheet of corrugated iron resting on rough unpainted wooden posts. Although the gust had given way to the general lessening of the wind, the oil lantern suspended from a bracket swung gently. The bench had been deserted by the superannuated fishermen sucking at their clay pipes; doubtless even they had been discouraged by the driven spume that glistened on every surface.

He sat down. Apparently the shelter was not used only by the old. On the wall against which he leaned he had read, scribbled in school chalk, 'Paddy Flynn loves Maggie O'Driscoll — TRUE. Mike Slattery loves Pegeen Fitzgerald — TRUE. In one case the swain had attempted to scribble out his name, but not so the young lady. How were his father and mother faring? How would they fare? Perhaps, after painful months, his father would break down, and his mother would find forgiveness at the horrifying sight. Perhaps a scapegoat would be found; Jenny must have thrown herself at his head.

Jim recalled the time when, planting a row of onions, he had inadvertently set one of the bulbs upside down. When later he dug it up, it was to find that the roots, on emerging from the top, had immediately turned downwards in the tenacious drive to fulfil their function; while the stem, issuing from the bottom, had climbed its way upwards into the light of the sun. So also with his father and mother. Their marriage would go on because they both understood the art of life; the art of makedo and mend. It was only the purists, in their brittle strength, who broke and perished.

He rose and stood at the front of the shelter, watching the dying storm. Yes, the padre was right. Time healed. Jenny and he would make their way through life together. So at last he had found love! Or, rather, he had found out that he had had it all along. Love was needing someone, and serving them.

The harbour waters were turgid with mud churned up from the sea bed. Brown swaths of seaweed, flecked with yellow and white foam and harried by gusts of wind, drifted in like torn-up hopes, and the clouds were melting away like dreams that had died. The long black fishing-boats would again sleep on still harbour waters.

Returning, he climbed up to his studio and looked out of the window. The golden companies of the heavens marshalled themselves and shone, producing stillness out of their eternal fiery nuclear exchange, a savage crucible manufacturing serenity.

He picked up his brush.

Up at Karachi House Henry stood in his pyjamas and dressing-gown at his bedroom window. Behind him was the bed, packed with hot-water bottles, in which his wife supposed that he was lying. She herself was down in the kitchen preparing soup.

So Jenny was refusing to marry Jim! Strange girl! She had her dignity though. Of course he'd help her mother and her with money. It was the only thing in which he wasn't bankrupt. But how would it all end?

He noted that the storm was already blowing itself out. The schooner and the trawlers, silent, secret, aloof, lay more quietly at their moorings. The moon careered through such wisps of cloud as remained. The strange half-light flickered, now strengthening, now dying, as at some primal dawn upon the threshold of creation: upon the distant bastion of King William Fort at whose foot he had so nearly perished; over the roof tops of Lower Glenmorris where dwelt the son whom he might have taken with him into the cold embrace of the harbour waters; over the obscure bulk of the Glenmorris Printing Company, that red-brick temple in which he had served and where he must serve amidst the whispers to the end, for he was too old now to begin again; and back once more to the distant shores of the outer harbour where the gulls had started crying; where the siren buoy, rising and falling on the sea-mountains running in, moaned at its lonely station; where were the grasses, and the groves, and the lazy autumn stream now swollen into winter flood, where it had all begun.

A lone seagull winged its way past. Its cry was filled with the wild desolation of craggy abodes and the uncertainty of a livelihood filched savagely from grey heaving waters.

He turned away from the window to face life anew.

END

THE BLACK AN' TAN

The Black an' Tan

'Tis quare things dreams are,' said the old man, shaking his head slowly. 'Sometimes there'd be a lot in thim, and then agin there'd be nothin' at all. They say that Julius Caesar would never have been murdered if he'd listened to his wife, and stayed at home. I call to mind, now, some such kind of a dream of warnin' as came to Julius Caesar's wife. Only this time the dream was heeded, and them that had it was saved, but not in the way that they'd be expectin'.' The old man chuckled. 'No, sir, not by any means in the way that they'd be expectin.'

'At the time that this dream came to the two auld sisters, who lived in that lonely house that you see on the hill yon, they was both gettin' a little strange in their ways, what with being alone the way that they was. 'Twas no one they had belongin' to them. Their mother, God rest her, had long since departed this life; and their father, a few years back, had fallen head first down the shaft of a diamond mine he part owned in Africa, and crowned hisself with more than a tiara.

'Once a week only, the two sisters would be after walking into the village in their shabby auld black clothes, to get whatever they'd need at Mr Harvey's store. Judith, the elder, was already white and wrinkled. Mary, a bit younger looking, was held be them to have been the beauty, because a man had once looked at her. He was wondering why she didn't shave off her moustache, but no matter.

'Well, on the morning of the day I'm talkin' of ('twas during the time of The Troubles), the two sisters came down to breakfast each looking as white as if she'd been after seeing a man.

' "What's ailin' you, Mary?" says the elder of them.

' "I'm after havin' a terrible dream, Judith."

133

' "Dream!" says Judith, nearly leppin' out of her skin. "'Tis meself is after having a dream too."

'And then the whole thing comes out. Them two dreams is exactly the same, aye, even to the smallest thing.'

The old man shook his head triumphantly. 'Now did ye ever hear the like of that, sir, or read of it in any book? 'Tis impossible for two people to have exactly the same dream; isn't that what you're sayin' to yourself? Yet 'tis the truth I'm tellin' you, and any man or woman in the village will tell you the same, for the story is still a wonder round these parts.

'Well, the two sisters sat for a while starin' at one another, and then Judith says, "Mary, we must have our money put in the bank at once."

' "We'll get Mr Harvey to do it for us," says Mary. "He's a business man and understands these things."

' "Now ladies," says Mr Harvey when he has taken them into the private office at the back of the store, "what can I do for you?" He had a kind heart in him, had Mr Harvey, though a trifle strict and dignified in his ways, seeing that he was a big man in the parish. Yes, sir, 'tis next to the priest hisself I'd say he was.

' "Well, Mr Harvey," says Judith, being, as you might say, the leader, though the pair of them was as timid as a man askin' his wife for the price of a drink, "me and my mister has had a terrible dream."

' "Oh!" says Mr Harvey, astonished.

' "Yes," says Mary, "and we want you to help us to put all our money in the bank."

' "Why certainly, m'am," he says, affable like. "And what sort of a bit of an amount would it be?"

' "Thirty thousand pounds," says Judith.

' "What!" says Mr Harvey, nearly falling out of his hard wooden chair (for he was a hardy man and wouldn't give hisself no comforts).

' "Our father's share of the diamond mine," says Mary.

' "What class of a dream was it you had, m'am?" he says mopping his forehead, for he felt fair certain them two sisters was mad, but was just a small bit afraid it might be hisself.

' "Well, 'tis like this," says Judith. "Me and my sister dreamt we was alone in the house listenin' to the storm raging outside, when we heard a knockin' at the door. We went to see who it was at all, and there, standin' on the doorstep, was an English soldier (a Black an' Tan too he was), and him drippin' with the rain. And in he comes with never a word, and goes straight to the loose plank in the parlour, and lifts it up and takes the money, and then he murders the two of us."

' "Well well," says Mr Harvey, relieved like, for he was beginnin' to think maybe them sisters was sane after all, because he'd heard tell before of auld women what would keep a pile in the house, and they livin' like paupers. "That was a pretty terrible class of a dream sure enough, m'am. And both of yez to have the very same! That was an astonishing thing, now!"

'After thinkin' a bit he said, "Sure, ladies, you know right well there's not a thing in the wide world that I wouldn't do to help yez, for 'tis good customers of mine ye are. But I'm afraid," says he, "that we'll have to postpone the bankin' of the money till Monday, for today is Saturday, and the bank will be closing in five minutes."

' "Then will you keep it for us in your safe?" says Judith.

' "Ah, I'm afraid, m'am, I couldn't make meself responsible for a sum the like o' that. But sure, 'tis been safe there this long while, and it will be safe there this wee while longer."

'So with that they had to rest content, but they spent the day listenin' to the wind roaring in the chimney, and they didn't eat so much as one potato. And sure, be the time they went off to their beds, they was that jumpy they'd lep at the sound of the kitten makin' water on the carpet.

'They hadn't been shiverin' in their beds an hour, listenin' to the rain slappin' at the window, when, begob, didn't they hear a loud knockin' at the door!

' "What's that?" says Mary, sittin' up with her back rigid and her eyes wide and glazed, as though a man had proposed to her.

' "Hush," says Judith from under the bedclothes. "Don't take no notice, and maybe he'll go."

'The words were hardly out of her mouth, when the knockin' came again.

'Well, the two of them lay there for the space of time that it would take yourself to lower two glasses of porter, listening to the knocking, and the man's voice calling above the howling of the storm for food and shelter.

'And at last them two sisters could stand it no longer. So Judith turns up the lamp, which they had kept lighted. Then she takes a poker in her hand and, with Mary following and the kitten weavin' in and out of her legs and nearly trippin' her, she goes downstairs and unlocks the door. A terrible blast o' wind blows it open in her face and puts out the lamp. But the second before the lamp goes out, sure enough they sees a Black an' Tan standin' right in the doorway. Drenched to the skin he was, and the face of him fierce and hungry-lookin' as a tax-collector's. He had a rifle across his back, and a bayonet hangin' be his side.

'Mary lets a yelp out of her and collapses like a concertina at the end of a jig.

' "What's it yer after wantin'?" stammers Judith, her knees knockin' like an auld bachelor's when he sees a widow woman's eye on him.

' "Food and shelter, lady," says the soldier, coming in and closing the door. "Give me your lamp," says he, "and I'll light it for you."

'He had some dry matches in his pocket and he lights the lamp. He lifts Mary into the parlour and gives her a taste o' whiskey out of a bottle he has.

'Well, sir,' said the old man, 'that Black an' Tan finished the whole of a dry loaf as happy as a fellah beatin' up his mother- in-law. And all the time he was eating, he kept starin' at the two women, but divil a word out of him.

'Well, after he's done, Judith plucks up her courage and asks him whether he's far to go.

' "Go!" says he. "Why, lady," says he, "I 'oped I might spend the blinkin' night 'ere. You wouldn't send a bloke out on a night like this, eh?"

'After a bit of hagglin', 'twas agreed that the Black an' Tan is to spend the night where he was, and the two sisters is to take his rifle and bayonet up with them to their room. But they hadn't been in bed as long as 'twould take a newly landed sailor to find hisself a girl, expectin' any moment to be murdered, when they heard a noise at the front door. After a few more minutes, they heard footsteps coming quietly up the stairs.

' "Are you awake, ladies?" says the voice of the Black an' Tan.

' "I am," stammers Judith. "What's it you want?"

'Mary was gabblin' prayers like a man with money on a horse.

' "There's someone at the front door," says the soldier, "and I think it must be a burglar."

' "What will I do at all?" says Judith.

' "Give me my bayonet," says he, "and I'll open the door and see who it is."

' "No, please," whimpers Mary. "We'll give you money."

' "I don't understand you, miss," says he. "I only want to protect you in return for your kindness to me."

'Well, after a bit of persuadin' he gets the two of them to come out in their nightdresses, as slowly as a man handin' over the wages. Judith is holding the bayonet and Mary the lamp, and the three of them creep downstairs. And, begob, sure enough as they come down they hear a strange scrapin' class of a noise, and then they see somethin' glistening in the door. As they get closer, they see the thing is going backwards and forwards, and at the same time slowly moving round the lock.

' " 'Tis a class of a saw," whispers Judith.

' "Give me my bayonet," says the Black an' Tan, "and stand back."

'Then he suddenly pulls open the door, lettin' in a terrible draught and blowin' out the lamp on them. But they all see a man standing outside, and the soldier goes out after him. Presently they hear a howl, like from a man that's had his face slapped in the back row at the pictures. When the soldier has returned agin and lighted the lamp, he shows them the bayonet all covered with blood.

' "He got away, ladies," says he, "but he took with him a ripped trousers seat, and maybe more than his trousers ripped. And now we can all go to bed," says he, "and I don't think you need worry that you'll be disturbed again."

'And sure enough, they spent the rest of that night in peace. In the mornin' the Black an' Tan, after a cup o' tea, thanked them and took hisself off, and never a coin did he take, and the money right in the room with him.

'Well, sir,' said the old man, laughing immoderately and slapping his thigh, 'when the two sisters went round to Mr Harvey's house that very same mornin', to insist that he keep their money for them till the bank opened on Monday, didn't Mrs Harvey herself come to the door and say that himself was terrible sick with the fluenzy, and couldn't be after seein' anyone.'

The old man fixed me with a piercing eye. ' 'Twas a week before anyone saw Mr Harvey at the store agin — and then he walked in limpin'. Well, maybe he got the fluenzy in the leg. But tell me this, sir. Why should a hardy man, that all his business life has sat on a hard wooden chair in his office, suddenly take to sittin' hisself down on the fattest, softest cushion in the furniture department? 'Tis nobody ever got to the bottom' — and here he permitted himself a wink — 'of that.'

THE STRANGE
IMPERFECTION OF
LI TSUNG

The Strange Imperfection of Li Tsung

During my writing days in Chelsea, I used to read and study the very many purely short-story magazines that then flourished; and that, not long afterwards, disappeared so catastrophically one after the other. The two authors in whom I took a special delight were P.G. Wodehouse and Ernest Bramah, the latter with his amusing pseudo-Chinese stories. Only later, when I was editing and publishing my monthly magazine *Commentary* during five and a half years in Dublin, did the idea occur to me that I too could compose a pseudo-Chinese story on the same lines. I published it in 1941 in the first issue of *Commentary*, and again five years later in one of the last. Nearly twenty years on, I gave it a third publishing in my quarterly magazine *Writing*, after the latter had been in existence for some six years. Now, and here, it receives a fourth.

In the dynasty of Chang flourished a rich merchant, Li Tsung. He was young and handsome, and possessed of all the moral and intellectual virtues, save one.

He loved Orange Blossom, the daughter of the enormously wealthy junk-owner, Wang Po. But his suit did not prosper on account of his one great fault. This fault was the more serious in a merchant, because it was calculated gravely to militate against his success in business matters. It certainly ruled him out as son-in-law and future heir to Wang Po.

One day Li Tsung went to the luxurious house of the junk-owner. He craved to be admitted to his presence.

'For what purpose, most excellent Li Tsung, do you come to see me?' enquired Wang Po politely. He squatted, his large ears sticking out fanwise from his head like those of the Emperor's state elephant, on a richly embroidered rug in the foremost chamber of his house.

Behind him stood his daughter, Orange Blossom. Her eyes, dark as the evening shadow cast by the summit of Wenn-yen, rested with favour upon the countenance of her suitor.

'I have come into your presence,' replied Li Tsung boldly, 'in order to mention once again the subject of your daughter.'

'He who speaks is curious to know what there is that you can add to your distinguished pleas, which of late have begun to weary him not a little.'

'Is it not true that I should stand in your regard as a fit husband for your daughter, were it not but for my one great fault?'

'It is true.'

'Then he who stands before you confidently demands her hand in marriage.'

Curiosity gleamed in the black slits of Wang Po's eyes. 'I'm all ears,' he said, speaking more truly than he supposed.

'But an hour ago a traveller from the North appeared in the town. He spoke of a distinguished ancient, one Sing, who dwells in singular discomfort in a cave but two days' journey hence. This Sing is possessed of all knowledge. He likewise can cure all faults of the spirit and the intellect.'

'It is your intention to seek a cure at his hands?'

'I leave within the hour, O most illustrious Wang Po.'

It was the second day. The sun, brighter than the golden chariot of the Emperor, was setting behind the summit of Wenn-yen.

Up the winding mountain path, borne on the shoulders of perspiring coolies, crawled a litter. Presently it paused before the yawning jaws of a mighty cavern. At the mouth of the cavern stood an ancient with a white beard that reached to his knees. From the litter descended Li Tsung.

'It is this person's not unreasonable conjecture,' he observed, 'that you are the talented ancient, Sing.'

The old man bowed his head in a low obeisance of assent, so that his beard touched his toes.

'He who speaks is Li Tsung, possessed of all the moral and intellectual virtues, save one. Should your renowned capabilities prove adequate to cure him of his fault, he will reward you with a not inconsiderable quantity of cash.'

'I have sufficient cash for my few needs, Li Tsung,' replied Sing. 'What is your fault?'

'My intellect has, as it were, a great gap in it. I can remember nothing.'

'He who stands before you wonders whereby you have remembered the thousand and one matters that appertain to a journey.'

The young merchant sat down on a boulder in the opening of the cave and pondered. At last he said, 'My memory has two sides to it, even as the image of the Buddha in the temple has two eyes. All that appertains to Pleasure, be it Love, or Feasting, or Wine, will my memory most tenaciously hold. But all that appertains to Business, be it an agreement to meet such and such a merchant in the market-place, or to attend the lading of a junk with merchantise at such and such an hour; these things can I in no wise remember.'

Sing concealed a smile. 'Your only fault is that you are young.'

'Nay, 'tis a serious fault. I would be free of all fault.'

'Then I fear you may, perchance, find yourself free of all virtue too,' remarked Sing with gravity. 'The character of a man is a picture, painted by the cunning hand of an artist. In everything there is a balance preserved. Every light has its shadow.'

'Your profound meaning is, that there is no such division of characteristics as that into good and evil?'

'This person means no more, my son,' replied the ancient a trifle sententiously, 'than that every nature has its compensations. Thus the brave man is sometimes reckless, and the cautious a coward. The man of industry and business acumen often times forgets the purpose of cash and becomes a miser. Another man is a spendthrift and a profligate, but at the same time generous and warm-hearted.'

'Your implication is, that he who reforms a fault loses its brother virtue?'

The ancient heaved a sigh. 'I fear it is sometimes so.'

For a moment Li Tsung hesitated. Then the vision of Orange Blossom flooded his mind, and he knew that he would, to be cured of his fault, even be willing if necessary to incur the displeasure of his Ancestors.

Sing read his thoughts. 'You are freed from your fault,' he said, stretching out his withered hand and touching him upon the forehead.

Li Tsung leapt up, as though he had been bitten by some ill-disposed mosquito. He ran to the litter. 'Make haste,' he called to the bearers.

'This audacious outcast vainly conjectures as to the distinguished reason, which has led you so abruptly to withdraw your harmonious features from his sight,' remarked the ancient with ill-concealed curiosity.

'The venerable moustaches of my Ancestors be praised,' cried Li Tsung, as his bearers bore him away. 'I have but now recollected a meeting of the merchants in the market-place, which I must needs attend before the sun sets tomorrow over Wenn-yen.'

From sunset to sunrise journeyed Li Tsung, using relays of coolies, and then almost to sunset again. Presently he entered the town where he dwelt. As he was borne hastily along, one called to him by name. It was the junk-owner, Wang Po, who stood in front of his house, his fan-like ears red in the rays of the great sky-lantern. Before him were his bearers with a gorgeous litter.

'Whither do you hasten, O Li Tsung?' he cried. 'The tavern is behind you!'

'This person hastens to the conference of merchants in the market-place.'

The black slits of Wang Po's eyes almost opened wide, so distinguished was his astonishment. 'Return hither,' he called after the fast-disappearing Li Tsung. 'There is yet much time before the conference. Rest and wash yourself, and this person will accompany you to the market-place.'

'Do as he bids,' said the young merchant to his bearers.

'Has Sing, the ancient, worked a wonder, that your auspicious memory had deigned to remember the negligible conference?' enquired Wang Po, as he ushered Li Tsung into the foremost chamber of his house, where sat the harmoniously proportioned Orange Blossom, embroidering a fan.

'May the growth of his beard prosper!' replied the young merchant with well-bred enthusiasm. 'He has restored my memory to me.'

'The arrested development of this undesirable person's intellect makes it difficult for him to believe so astonishing a thing. Nevertheless it must be so, else would you now have been honouring the tavern with your dignified, if hilarious, presence.'

144

He signed to Orange Blossom, who had risen to her feet on their entry, to advance. He took his daughter by the hand and turned to the young merchant. 'The word of Wang Po has gone forth. She is yours. Take her to be your wife.'

Li Tsung blinked. 'She is more desirable than a lantern in the time of no light,' he said softly. 'Who is she? What is her name?'

JAPAN

Japan

Sun-goddess emperor, Kyoto-born.
Imperial warriors armed with iron swords —
An iron death inlaid with work of gold —
Sword-belted samurai that strode the streets.
High feudal castles rear amidst the town,
Small houses, bare and comfortless, beneath,
Where sliding paper screens divide the space,
Stark houses brightened by those painted screens.
Corners alone make okimona-bright,
Birds, dragons, crayfish, wondrous to the sight.

The giant Buddha broods by Nata's wall.
Sand gardens, dry, in temples Zen abound.
Weddings and births in Shinto shrines — but death
In funeral fires torch-lighted Buddhist-wise.
Zen priests that paint Sung china — do they still?
Carved wood and metal fill the temple carved,
Bells, vases, lanterns, candlesticks in bronze,
And ivory vies with wood.
Kano simplicity and colour vie,
And temples, shrines, padogas search the sky.

Buffoloes roam, back-grounded by sharp hills,
Once-fiery Fugi, now snow capped, asleep,
Hot-water Honshu springs still steam the air,
And Ishikari and Shinano flow.
Typhoons yet tear the towns and tear the tides,

But dykes great Tokio and Osaka save,
The bullet train Osaka-Tokio bound.
Kitakyusha forging mighty steel,
Rice fields that ripple in the summer air,
Mulberry for silk. Textiles, ceramics, toys.
Tea-ceremony courtesans bow low.
The lovers sitting, cherry trees above,
At night, by lacquered lakes, find lantern love.

MAD WITH MABEL

Mad with Mabel

Two cyclists went out riding together. After a time the first cyclist dismounted and let all the air out of his back tyre. 'Why did you do that?' enquired the second cyclist. The first cyclist replied, 'Because my saddle was too high and I wanted to lower it.' 'Give me a wrench,' said the second cyclist. He loosened his handlebars, turned them back to front, and tightened them up again. 'Why did you do that?' asked the first cyclist. 'I'm going home,' said the second cyclist. 'I'm not going out riding with a fool like you.'

So began my editorial for the August 1959 issue of *Writing*, at that time entitled *S. D's Review*. 1959 was the year of the magazine's inception. My Manuscript Society had been set up two years earlier. Four years before that, we had moved into the cottage.

When my wife Margaret and I took up residence, with our children Paul, Edwina and Madeleine, the cottage was completely empty except for six pounds and ten shillings' worth of furniture, including an iron bed, bought from the previous owners, a retired engine driver and his wife. Our own possessions consisted mainly of books and pictures. The books originated from the small library of novels, mainly Victorian, that I had formed with my schoolboy pocket-money while at St Columba's College; and the somewhat larger library of poetry, plays, belles-lettres and biographies acquired while at Worcester College, Oxford. At a later date the collection was enlarged with volumes selected from my mother's library, left to me in her will, including first editions of all the works of her youngest brother, and my uncle and godfather, the dramatist Dr Lennox Robinson, late director of the Irish national theatre, the Abbey Theatre in Dublin. The pictures, presents from artist friends, had their origins in a gallery which Margaret ran in Dublin for a year, later augmented by gifts from Margaret's sister, the artist Pepi Gillies.

As being the cheapest way of covering the floors, we bought mats. The considerable areas between their edges and the walls were filled with a liberal use by Margaret of 'liquid lino', applied to the floor with a paint brush. Even now, when every room has been wall-to-wall carpeted, a large sprinkling of attractive mats remain. In fact, the cottage may be said to be pictures, books and mats.

And clocks. We have twelve of them of various sorts: clocks that strike the hour, clocks that strike the half hour as well, a clock that chimes the quarters and strikes the hour, clocks that just tick loudly and cheerfully and are content to tell the time to the nearest five to ten minutes. Margaret led the way by acquiring them from acquaintances selling up their houses to move elsewhere, and I have followed her lead by further purchases since her death. A local clock man would talk to me only in terms of cold silent chronometers, stressing that they would keep the time to within a second in the year. Finally I was obliged to put my foot down, and silence him by roundly pointing out that a clock is not a timepiece. A clock is a carnival.

The August 1959 issue of *S. D.'s Review* was not the first. The first was the January issue of that year, under the extremely dull title of *The Magazine*, a title that was changed with the second issue. But it was the one which saw the publication of the short story, *Mad With Mabel*. While sitting in a dentist's waiting-room, I picked up a magazine. To keep my mind off the coming ordeal, I turned to the 'joke' page. I copied out the best of the jokes. When I got home, I set myself the challenge of stringing them together to form a coherent story. Here is the result.

Mind you, my wife's the most wonderful woman in the world. And that isn't just my opinion. It's hers too. Curves? I call her Poppa's Meat Ration. Cook? You have to fix lead weights to her pastry before you start to eat it, or it would float away.

Then why did her first husband, fifteen stone and fond of the trencher, leave her eight years ago and run away to sea? Why am I making a get-away too, after only a year of marriage?

After Fat Bill, as he was known to his mates, had vanished for seven years, and she was legally entitled to presume him dead, she took me to husband. And 'took' is the word.

I hadn't been married to her three weeks, before I began to see what my dad meant when he led me aside and said, 'Son, if ever your wife should ask you whether you're a man or a mouse, don't be afraid. Squeak right up.' Then there was the day when I overheard her saying to a woman friend, 'My old man has a mind of his own. Luckily, he never uses it.'

It was things like that began to get me down, that and the sweet eating. Seems, when Fat Bill walked out on her, her nerves went to pieces. She had to have something in her mouth all the time, and it was a choice between sweets and cigarettes.

'Keep off cigarettes,' her doctor had said, 'they kill the appetite and you won't eat properly. You'll lose weight. You'll get thin. You'll become skin and bone. You'll end up a scarecrow. Look at me! I smoke seventy a day.'

He had patted her shoulder with a trembling hand. She had supported him over to the surgery couch, then gone out and bought a pound of sweets. Gobstoppers.

Then this row blew up, and that finished it. She was church mad. She would sit listening to the sermon, her eyes rolling in her head and a gobstopper rolling in her mouth. First she got me made a Select Vestryman. Then a Sidesman. Then it was the Scouts. Finally, when the electrical pumping gear of the organ broke down in the middle of the service, she had me rush up and work the hand pump. And me with my lumbago! I'll never forget the hymn, *Onward, Christian Soldiers*. By the time we got to the last verse, I was a battle casualty.

After that, I was darned if I was going to look after a stall at the forthcoming church bazaar. Whereupon she started screaming at me. The gobstopper flew out of her mouth and hit the cat in the eye. 'And what's more,' were her last bitter words, 'I would never have married you if you hadn't tried so hard to get away.'

It was true. I *had* tried to get away. A pal had warned me that Fat Bill had married her for her cooking and left her for her temper. But Mabel just wobbled her curves at me, gave me a steak that melted in the mouth — and took me to husband.

Well, I was getting out now, and quick. I jammed my hat on my head and picked up my suitcase.

As I walked down the street, I caught the tones of a sargeant instructor coming from an army hut. 'Your rifle is your best friend.

Take every care of it. Treat it as you would your wife, and rub it all over every day with an oily rag.'

I shouldn't have minded rubbing Mabel with an oily rag. It might have made her grate less. Well, the next best thing was to go and get oiled myself.

Trouble is, I'm not a drinking man. I once had half a glass of elder-berry wine with a maiden aunt to cheer her up after the death of her canary. I wouldn't know what to order.

I turned into a hotel. There was a long room, with respectable-looking people sitting around between palms in pots and talking quietly. A few sat on stools at a bar in one corner.

I ordered a double Scotch. They always ordered double Scotches in the stories I had read. They say that drinking makes you see double and feel single. The latter was okay with me, as long as I didn't see a double vision of Mabel. Not that a double vision of Mabel would fit into any normal sized room.

I put back the double Scotch. Things began to go the other way round. I began to feel double — like double-crossing Mabel; and see single — girls.

There was one sitting quite near me. She had hair the colour of ripe corn and forget-me-not blue eyes, like all the girls in the books I read who married the blokes who ordered the double Scotches.

What was it that my father had told me? You have reached middleage when a girl you smile at thinks you know her. Well, I was getting thin on top, but I had to make sure. I ordered and sank another double Scotch. I smiled. She smiled. Good Lord, I *did* know her. She was the vicar's daughter.

I couldn't get out of it. I had to go over to her table and give her a neighbourly greeting. I staggered slightly. I frowned angrily at the carpet, to make her suppose that I had tripped over a passing woodworm. I sat down hurriedly opposite her, and couldn't get up again.

In no time she had me in conversation about the forthcoming church bazaar. Seems she was to be in charge of the cooking in the refreshment tent. This led to that, and in the end I felt it my duty to suggest some form of entertainment. Something high-toned, of course.

156

'There's an exhibition of photographs of church organs at the Seaman's Institute. Would you care to accompany me to view them?'

'Church organs, baloney!' laughed Cecile (for so she had been named by her uncle, the Bishop of Bognor Regis, at her christening some twenty summers back). 'In her time off, it's bubbly and rock an' roll for this baby.'

'Very well.' I stood up, and at once collapsed.

Cecile picked me up and took my arm, a thoughtful look in her forget-me-not blue eyes. 'They make the floors of these licensed hotels so uneven,' she murmured.

So we cut a rug at a low dock-side joint where we judged that she would be unlikely to run into her uncle, the Bishop.

We sat out the next one, and I told Cecile my troubles. 'And I'm going to run away to sea, like Fat Bill,' I concluded, raising my voice.

We noticed that there was a lean hollow-cheeked chap sitting at the next table, with a seaman's cap at his elbow. That is, we noticed what we could see of him. His head was buried in a cloud of smoke from his own pipe. He seemed to be in eruption.

He leaned across to me. 'My name is Captain William Fenton.'

He spat, missing the headwaiter by the width of a bottle-opener and hitting a parrot in a cage. The parrot made two remarks of which the Bishop wouldn't have approved, and a third which he wouldn't have understood.

'Couldn't help hearing your final remark that you were looking for a sea berth,' said Captain Fenton. 'Well, as it happens, I want a hand for my fishing trawler, *The Jellied Eel*. What can you do?'

'Well,' I stammered, 'I can — I can —'

'Fine. Fine. Just the man I need. I'm on my way to *The Jellied Eel* now. You'd better come straight aboard.'

I said goodbye to Cecile She advised me earnestly to get myself a wife in every port. 'You'll need it for your Seaman's Certificate.'

'I'll be sailing tomorrow,' said Captain Fenton, as we made our way to the dock. 'But first I've a call to make on a slim little baggage in town. She's as trim and slender a craft as ever tied up alongside a seaman's jetty.'

Supper was served at once on board. After I had broken two teeth on a ship's biscuit, and drunk a cup of tea that tasted of jellied eels

157

and tar, I knew that I wanted to go back to Mabel. I'd been with her too long to be able to do without her wonderful cooking.

But before I could walk ashore, my head banged on the table. I was asleep. The double Scotches, not to mention the bubbly, had been too much for a chap used to half glasses of elder-berry wine.

When I woke next morning, it was to find myself in one of the trawler's bunks. Voices came from the little stateroom next door. One of them was Mabel's.

I staggered out. I was still in my clothes. I half fell into the stateroom. There was Mabel, sitting on Captain William Fenton's knees. I could hear the bones of his legs creaking under the weight. Behind them was an untouched breakfast of jellied eels.

'This is my long-lost Fat Bill,' cried Mabel, embracing the emaciated scarecrow. 'He had changed his surname.'

'And this is my trim little craft,' cried Fat Bill, making a hopeless attempt to put his arm round Mabel's waist. 'No more jellied eels for your truly. It's back to Mabel and her steaks.'

Seems, after he ran away from her, his nerves went to pieces. He had to have something in his mouth all the time, and it was a choice between cigarettes and sweets.

'Keep off sweets,' his doctor had said. 'You'll put on weight. You'll become enormous. Look at me. I eat a pound of gobstoppers a day.'

Fat Bill had supported the medicine man over to the surgery couch, which had immediately collapsed under him. Then he had gone out and bought a pouch of tobacco. Shag.

So I wasn't married to Mabel after all! I stumbled out. I crossed the gangway to the quay. I wandered through the town for hours.

I heard a band. Perhaps it would cheer me up. It was the church bazaar.

'Hie, yer!'

It was the voice of Cecile, who was in charge of the cooking arrangements in the refreshment tent.

I told her my story.

She disappeared, and reappeared with an omelette. It melted in the mouth. She wobbled her curves at me . . .

KILLED WITH A SOFT
INSTRUMENT

Killed With a Soft Instrument

You would never have thought that little old Tom, his white hair ruffled by the sea breeze as he leaned over his back garden fence, was planning murder on account of a women.

For more than thirty years he had, of an evening, leaned over at precisely this spot, where there was a gap in the hedge growing along just inside the fence. He had made and maintained the gap there on purpose. His garden ended on the very edge of the cliff, and through the gap he got a wonderful view of the sea, breaking in surf on the rocks far below.

On either hand, sweeping round the Cornish bay, was the line of rock and clay cliff, here and there deeply eroded by wind and rain. From a natural platform half way down the cliff, to his left, came the beat of a small pumping engine. He could see the engine hut, its door as usual left open.

It was a backward part of the county, with no piped-in public water supply to the houses. The pumping engine was started up, when needed, to fill the salt-water tanks of the big house on whose land old Tom's cottage stood. There were many jobs for which the sea-water could be used, to spare the rain-water collected off the roof. Drinking water had to be fetched from the village pump.

Without shifting his position, except to turn his head to the right, old Tom could see old Harry, the man he was going to kill. Tom was five feet five inches in height; Harry was six foot two. Tom weighed nine and a half stone; Harry had fifteen stone in quite fair condition. Yet Tom felt sure of his ability to kill Harry.

Harry's cottage was next to Tom's, to which it was joined. Harry's back garden was separated from Tom's only by a fence. Harry's garden ended in a bed of hollyhocks, beyond which was the hedge.

Harry had made no gap in his hedge. He didn't seem to feel a need to gaze across the sea of an evening. But then, *he* had no cause to eat out his heart, to dream dreams. *He* had had the reality. *He* had been married to Nora.

Tom ran his fingers exasperatedly through his thick white hair, as he watched Harry's bald head bowed over the hollyhocks he was tending. Thinking of Nora he would be; she loved hollyhocks, and he had originally planted the bed for her.

Every evening, as Tom gazed across the sea, at the same time watching Harry out of the corner of his eye, Harry would be there, tending his hollyhocks. More like *caressing* than tending them! As if they were Nora! Perhaps Harry too was eating out his heart now and dreaming his dreams. For Nora was dead.

Tom remembered the time when, in their thirties, they had both been courting Nora. Both had been working in the same china-clay pit Bodmin way.

One day little Tom had been standing at the quarry face, directing a powerful jet at it from the hose, and washing down the mixed china stone and china clay. The china clay flowed away in gullies to the tanks to settle, leaving the coarser china stone behind.

He had looked up to see the stalwart form of Harry making his way down the steep pyramid of china-stone reject, which reared up against the sky. As he descended, Harry prevented himself from slipping by placing the soles of his boots carefully against the sleepers of the narrow-guage rails running up the side of the pyramid.

He had been working on the rails and sleepers. He had clever hands, had Harry. When it came to carpentry, or any form of engineering, he was a wizard. He could fix anything.

Harry had walked straight up to Tom.

'D'you think Nora will like this?' he had said, grinning maliciously.

He had opened his huge palm. Tom had stared at it. He was always fascinated by Harry's hands: their strength, their flexibility, their uncanny skill. But he had had a special reason for staring that day. For he had caught the glint of a diamond.

'What is it, man? Is it — is it an engagement ring?'

'Aye.'

'Oh. Congratulations.'

'Thanks.'

162

Nora had come to live with Harry next door. The agony of seeing her strolling with him in his garden had almost driven Tom out of his mind. One day, when Harry was out, and Nora came into the garden alone, Tom had poured out to her the story of his pain.

She had taken his face between the palms of her hands, as though he were a child, and kissed him. 'You have lovely thick black hair, Tom,' she had said. 'I always admired it.'

The agony had hardly grown less, for he had known that it was merely a kiss of comfort. As to his hair, there was little else that she could have said. It was his sole good feature.

Time had dulled the pain, but never stilled it. Yet, for Nora's sake, he had allowed Harry to go on living. He could not have killed him without grieving her. It was grief enough to her that she had never had a child.

Three months ago, Nora had died.

Tom studied Harry as he bent over the hollyhocks. He would kill him while he was in his garden, just where he was now. There would be no crossing of the fence, no tell-tale stealthy tiptoes in the clay soil. There would be no bullet hole; Tom had no firearms. There would be no wound from a thrown blade; Tom possessed nothing more formidable than a bread-knife badly in need of sharpening. There would be no bruises from a club or any other hard instrument.

No, the instrument that Tom would use would be the softest imaginable, softer than Nora's kiss, and even more terrible. It would be — water.

Harry turned round. Tom shifted his eyes away quickly, afraid lest Harry should see the hatred in them. He thought that Harry was still watching him. Was he becoming suspicious? No, that was nonsense.

Tom gazed across the sea. Yes, he would use water; ordinary everyday water. Salt water, actually. That was only because there was such a lot of it to hand. Oh, no no, he wasn't going to drown him! Nothing like that.

Well, while the daylight lingered, he had better familiarise himself once more with the route. He entered his cottage, came out on to the road by the front door, and made his way through the estate. He found the path which zig-zagged down the cliff face. In little over five minutes he was standing on the natural plaform beside the pump-house. The engine wasn't going. He peeped in through the ever-open door. There was no one inside.

He raised his eyes to the brow of the cliff; to the fence and the hedge running along the ends of Harry's and his gardens. The first thing that he saw was Harry looking down at him.

It was only for a moment. Harry had been there, and then Harry had not been there. But it was enough to make Tom break out into a sweat. For it meant that Harry knew that there was something up; knew it so well that he had actually crossed the fence between the two gardens to watch Tom through the gap in the hedge, the only place from which he could be seen.

When Tom got back to his cottage, he didn't go out into the garden. He went into his bedroom. Looking out cautiously, he saw Harry bowed once more over the hollyhocks. Then, setting his alarm clock to go off at four in the morning, he retired to bed.

At half past four, dressed, he went into his garden shed and took out a length of hose fitted with a nozzle. When he had done what he had to do, he would simply replace the hose. There was no reason why he should not possess it. What its purpose was he didn't know. It had been in the shed when the estate agent had leased him the house.

As he emerged from his front door, all was silent in Harry's cottage. Tom made his way through a sleeping world. There was plenty of light in the summer night sky.

He entered the pump-house. He substituted the hose in his hand for the rubber tubing that connected the outlet of the pump with the pipe up to the big house. He had ascertained beforehand that the hose was of the right bore. Not for nothing had he worked for years at the hoses in the china clay pits; he knew how to manage.

He started the engine. It was noisy, but not too noisy. The houses were not very close, and people should be asleep. As to the petrol and oil he used, their loss would never be noticed. These efficient little machines ran on a thimbleful.

He picked up the nozzle, which he had been careful to place outside. The water was gushing from it in a continuous powerful jet, and the hose had been writhing about like a serpent. With the skill of years of practice, he pinpointed the spot at the brow of the cliff just below Harry's portion of the fence and hedge. Steadily the jet ate out the soft clay, doing in minutes what the wind and the rain had done in years to other parts of the cliff. No one would notice. It would be just another case of cliff erosion.

When he shut off the engine, there was a neat hollow scoured under the extreme end of Harry's garden. Just enough strength of earth left to support a few hollyhocks. But if that silly fellow Harry went and added his fifteen stone . . .

Tom hastened home, draining the hose as he went. Any tell-tale dampness would soon dry up.

At nine he had breakfast, then watched from a window. When Harry emerged, he too went out into his garden. He didn't want to miss anything. He wanted to hear a scream ring in his ears that day.

It was evening before Harry began to move towards the holly-hocks. Tom took up his own accustomed position at the gap. This was it! He leaned over the fence, and gave a sigh of satisfaction.

There was a rending of wood. The whole fence seemed to give beneath him. He pitched forward. The surf at the foot of the cliff, breaking over boulders, came rocketing up towards him. A scream rang in his ears. It was his own.

Harry, on his way to the hollyhocks, paused. He listened with satisfaction. That would teach the little squirt not to kiss other men's wives, when he thought that the husband was out of the house. Oh, he *had* gone out that day, but he had come back for something that he had forgotten, and seen the whole thing from a window. He had said nothing. He wasn't going to let the little squirt know that he was jealous.

He should have done him in years ago. But, for Nora's sake, he hadn't. He fancied that she was rather fond of the little squirt; sometimes mentioned something about his having nice hair. That had hurt. He himself had gone thin on top very early. Well, he didn't think it was more than a mild flirtation, and Nora must have some outlet. She hadn't a lot in her life, what with no children.

But now Nora was dead — and so was the squirt. It had been easy enough to fix that fence so that no one would ever know. He had always had clever hands. He had had a scare though, when he had seen the squirt watching him from that platform down at

165

the pump-house. Though what he was doing down there, heaven alone knew.

Well, he had better report the — accident — to the police. But, dang it, he wouldn't let the squirt put him off his routine. He'd first water his hollyhocks — if it was the last thing he did.

END

Portrait of My Youth
Sean Dorman

Portrait of My Youth traces the earlier years of a remarkable Irish writer, Sean Dorman. The narrative, always lively, often extremely funny, sweeps the reader along on a bubbling current. There are fascinating glimpses of the British Raj in India as seen through a young child's eyes; of Algiers and Aden as seen through those of an older schoolboy; of student escapades at Oxford and in Paris in a more carefree era; of a visit to an extraordinary French family near Nice and Cannes: of sexual shenanigans in London's bohemian Chelsea; of difficulties with an alcoholic uncle famous as an Irish playwright; of meetings with literary and theatrical notables: E. M. Forster, Granville Barker, Sean O'Casey, John Betjeman, T. S. Eliot, Barry Fitzgerald, Dame Sybil Thorndike, W. B. Yeats, Laurence Olivier, Deborah Kerr.

'Delightful, humorous, full of marvellous observation.'
Colin Wilson

At the age of fourteen, in his first term at his public school, Sean Dorman was awarded a prize as the best prose writer in the school. He was the winner of an essay competition open to the public schools of Great Britain and Ireland. After graduating at Oxford, he worked as a freelance journalist in London, contributing articles to some twenty periodicals, and ghosting six non-fiction books for a publisher. For five and a half years he edited a theatrical and art magazine in Dublin, and for twenty-six years in England a magazine for writers. His three-volume hardback, *The Selected Works of Sean Dorman*, comprises autobiography, essays, novels, short stories and verse.

ISBN 0 9518119 9 1   1 Price £4.99

The Raffeen Press

Red Roses for Jenny
Sean Dorman

Red Roses for Jenny . . . What did they mean to her? A father's affection? Or a lover's desire? If they meant either to her, or both to her, then why did she throw them away? Did her mother come to hear of them? Or the wife of the man who gave them to her? And Jim, what did he think? He must have seen them, and surely he must have been disturbed. Was Jenny carrying a child, or was she not? If she were, could Jim succeed on containing the scandal and so protect his mother's feelings? Canon Moss, for all his funny ways, was wise. Was his wisdom sufficient to save them all? And, at the end of the long day, why did Jenny restore the red roses to her office desk again?

After the great success of Sean Dorman's autobiographical first novel, *Brigid and the Mountain*, initially, until revised, entitled 'Valley of Graneen' and, under that title, a Book Society Recommendation; also praised by *The Times Literary Supplement*, *The Irish Press*, *The Scotsman*, Australia's *Sydney Morning Herald*, *Irish Independent*, and many others; Mr Dorman took time off to acquire the technique of the non-autobiographical novel. The result is *Red Roses for Jenny*, with its vivid characters and driving speed of narrative. If the mountain scapes of *Brigid and the Mountain* are fine, no less fine are the seascapes of *Red Roses for Jenny*, with storm scenes as background to a love between a man and a woman no less stormy.

ISBN 0 9518119 7 5   Price £4.99

The Raffeen Press

The Madonna
Sean Dorman

'English life through Irish wit.'

Judy Summers, arrested by the sound of men's voices, paused on her way to visit The Madonna. Her cheap gay cotton dress fluttered about her shapely legs. Judy Summers liked men. She liked them very much. Also, it had become imperative that she should acquire a husband . . .

They were beside the little wayside shrine. George saw that Judy's eyes were fixed on the painted Mother cradling in her arms her painted Baby. 'The birth and the feeding have been a great strain on you, darling. Don't you think that Mark ought to go on to the bottle?' Judy was shaking her head vigorously. 'I'd give my life for Mark. I feel — I feel there's something in me of The Madonna.'

George went to Rose. She drew away in hurt pride. He broke down her resistance and swept her into his arms. 'Of course you didn't mean any harm, sweetheart. I've had a very upsetting letter from Judy. I love my wife. She's the mother of my son, but it's been a great strain. You've helped me keep my sanity.' He began to rain down kisses on her brow, her cheeks, her lips. Eyes closed, she held up her face to receive them.

'*The Madonna* reads as inevitably as does Tolstoy and bears out Eliot's, "In my end is my beginning." If it reaches its proper audience, it will be read with a mixture of discovery and relief. The novel is still alive!'
George Sully

ISBN 0 9518119 6 7   Price £4.99

The Raffeen Press

Physicians, Priests & Physicists
Sean Dorman

The most potent reason for Sean Dorman's writing this book arose from the existence of his magazine *Commentary*. This monthly appeared in Dublin in the forties during five and a half years. At an average of two thousand copies a month, he felt it to be a certaintly that copies still lurked in collections both public and private, even possibly in newspapers files, there to haunt him. In his youthful, pugnacity, had he somtimes overstated his ease and fallen into folly? If so, the only way out was to republish his essays or editorials, with inserted toning down remarks where such seemed needed.

The essays cover the subjects of: literary censorship; cancer, heart disease and arthritis-resisting diets and exercises, including exercises underwater in a hot bath (his wife suffered from arthritis of the hip, and died of smoking and alcohol-induced cancer); the existence or non-existence of God as found in the Bible; or in the discoveries about the universe as found in the work of scientists such as Aristotle, Ptolemy, Copernicus, Galileo, Kepler, Newton, Einstein (his Special Theory, and his General Theory, of Relativity, are explained in simple terms), and the somewhat later quantum mechanics, and the twistor and superstring theories. Other essays are entitled: 'How to Rear a Baby', 'The Adventures of Marriage', Jew and Gentiles'.

ISBN 0 9518119 1 6   Price £5.95

The Raffeen Press

The Strong Man
Sean Dorman

The Strong Man, a comedy in three acts, can lay no claims either to distinction or to having been performed on a stage. But it can claim to have been read by a considerable number of people who have reported that it caused them not only to smile but, on occasion, to laugh outright. Should something that has given rise to smiles, and even laughter, be left upon a shelf, or be entombed in a drawer? Of course not. It should be produced in a book. Also produced in this book are three theatre critiques. In days gone by, Ireland gave to literature great playwrights from that seeming hotbed of dramatic genius, Dublin University: William Congreve, George Farquhar, Oliver Goldsmith. Since then there have been: John Millington Synge, Samuel Beckett (both from the same university), William Butler Yeats, Oscar Wilde, Bernard Shaw, Sean O'Casey. Well known, but perhaps less well known than they ought to be, are Denis Johnston and Teresa Deevy. I have devoted a critique to each of them. Also to William Shakespeare, an Englishman, I'm told. The trouble with William Shakespeare, is that he has been allowed, unfortunately, to develop into a cult figure. Not only are his great plays produced, but his lesser pieces also are reverently laid out upon the stage, thus almost certainly denying many hours of theatre time to others with better work to offer. Such a lesser piece, here reviewed, is *Twelve Night*.

ISBN 0 9503455 6 3   Price £3.95

The Raffeen Press

Brigid and the Mountain
Sean Dorman

On my right was the mighty and bare peak of Mount Shanhoun, in shape and proportion an almost perfect pyramid. Brigid stood by the door watching me. She wore a plaid kerchief over her head and tied under her chin.

Agnes's buxom body might have become more buxom, as her mother Brigid alleged, yet secretly I was attracted by it. She was so compact, so rounded, so sturdy and vigorous, so shapely, yes, even graceful, as she moved rhythmically, as I had seen her one day weeding a field of potatoes.

Under its first title of 'Valley of Graneen', before a revision, *Brigid and the Mountain* was Recommended by the Book Society. *The Times Literary Supplement*, after a long review, summed up the book in the phrase, 'beautiful restraint'. *The Scotsman* wrote, 'His sketches are vivid and sincere. The physical aspects of the valley are described with remarkable clarity, and Mr Dorman is equally successful in his portraits of the inhabitants.' *The Sydney Morning Herald* wrote, in the course of a review of over two hundred words, 'These sketches of Donegal are delightful.' *Irish Independent*: 'Of his days in the valley, his friendships, and his talks, (Sean Dorman) has moulded a book of much charm. There is writing of grace and high degree . . . Withal, it is a notable book.' *Irish Press*: 'Sean Dorman brought with him a receptive mind, an artists's observant eye, and some writing materials. The result is . . . a very pleasant book.'

ISBN 0 9518119 8 3   Price £4.99

The Raffeen Press